ALLEMANN

Studies in Austrian Literature, Culture, and Thought

Translation Series

Alfred Kolleritsch

Allemann

Translated and with an Afterword
by
Paul F. Dvorak

ARIADNE PRESS
Riverside, California

Ariadne Press would like to express its appreciation to the Austrian Cultur
Institute, New York and the Bundeskanzleramt – Sektion Kunst, Vienna f
their assistance in publishing this book.

Translated from the German *Allemann*

Library of Congress Cataloging-in-Publication Data

Kolleritsch, Alfred, 1931-
Allemann / Alfred Kolleritsch : translated and with an afterwo
by Paul F. Dvorak.
p. cm. -- (Studies in Austrian literature, culture, and thoug
Translation series)
ISBN 1-57241-068-X
1. National socialism--Austria--Fiction. I. Dvorak, Paul F.
II. Title. III. Series.
PT2671.0418A65 1999
833'.914--dc21

98-48746
CIP

Cover Design:
Art Director, Designer: George McGinnis

270 Goins Court
Riverside, CA 92507

Printed in the United States of America.
ISBN 1-57241-068-X (paperback original)

Alfred Kolleritsch

I

Joseph Algebrand had to postpone his trip to Abano for several days, because a businessman from the neighboring town had died. A bond existed between Joseph and this man, who was more than ten years older. The man had known Joseph's father quite well and had actually been a friend of his. Joseph visited him often because the man had the gift of making the past come alive in the present and of illustrating through his story-telling—something he specifically intended—that nothing from the past is truly past but rather that it just continues to repeat itself in one way or another. Joseph never contradicted the storyteller. It was important to him to find out as much as he could about his father and to observe how the storyteller extracted his threads from the woven fabric of the whole. This man knew perfectly well that Joseph despised his version of history, one that had remained unaltered by National Socialism, even though he was willing to overlook it. Joseph had no need of the man's insight; to be sure, an apology or a display of remorse would not have excused his past, but rather would have drawn attention to it and thereby made it even more despicable. The blatant atrocities seemed to Joseph more appropriately associated with the victims; they marked the boundaries that tolerate no crossing. They also did not just sacrifice the victims to the whim of judgment, pardon, or understanding. The truth of which this man was a part was and is *one* truth, the *Movement* toward it was not the result of personal failure, but the emergence of the enemy, the catastrophe of intuition that brings time to a halt, and similarly the retreat of a person retreating from mankind and of a human being positioning himself in that condition.

The man gave a person cause to be on guard. The fact that he was important, helpful, industrious, and respectable in society's eyes from the end of the war until his death was not a contradiction. In spite of it all, he was no wolf in sheep's clothing. He was the dark and simultaneously illuminating witness for a participation and for a sharing in and contributing to that which seemed to Joseph more practical to avoid naming unequivocally than to give the appearance of explanations and to amass a myriad of details for these explanations. One does not illuminate what is vague and dark by explaining it. Joseph considered it more appropriate to leave alone what was dark and tangled rather than to allow it to disappear or merely to place it in the grasp of clear concepts. It was Joseph's wish, at least for the way he observed things, to leave the incomprehensible on the stage, in the air, in the realm of phenomena.

A heavy rain fell as Joseph rode to the cemetery. A day earlier, on All Saints' Day, Joseph had also visited the cemetery. Nowhere else did names and their power to latch themselves onto the present seem as close to him as on the gravestones. There they were again, the people he had known. No more distant than the living and often closer than those entering bearing flowers and wreaths. Joseph stuck candles into the ground and lit them. In front of the chapel in the middle of the cemetery he met a classmate from his grammar school days, a rich grain dealer, who, whenever Joseph met him, always mentioned that he provided better for the farmers than those who exploited them. The powerful man in his typical country-style coat also looked after the affairs of the veterans' fraternal organization by crafting interpretations of events that hobbled along behind the catastrophes, whose horror they tried to explain away out of existence. They released a glimmer of truth as if it were truth itself that glimmered.

He extended his hand to Joseph, took off his hat with the other, and, befitting the setting, said solemnly, "The ceremony this morning with the top brass of the SS at the cemetery of heroes was extraordinarily impressive." Forty-two years after the end of the war the sentence reverberated as it always had. It flowed from the man's very nature like a victory song, like the triumph of emotion over light. "Tomorrow you will see these officers at the interment."

When Joseph arrived at the cemetery, hundreds of people were already gathered around the grave; many had climbed up on gravestones in order to get a better view. The priest recited his prayers softly and raised his voice more distinctly only during the common prayers. Standing to the left and right of the deceased's relatives, who were dressed in their mourning outfits, were some large men and some noticeably short, stocky ones in gray coats. Almost all of them had bald pates from which the rain parted in rivulets. Despite the rain their coats remained open, the lapels of their jackets burgeoned with ribbons and medals. As if dug out of the grave along with the soil, they stood there, immutable, stonelike. The widow stood closest to the grave, as if sprouting out of the end of the rows these men formed as they lined up shoulder to shoulder. After the priest extended his hand to her and then retreated, her face beamed as the tallest of the men stepped forward from the row and began to speak over the dead man. The words struck home and gradually unleashed what lay bottled up within her: the time-honored truth enriched by the worship and power of its endurance. The reconstitution of the effective affective powers had created the load-bearing strength of an ideal, inviolable language, which made the futility of any other use of the great words evident. "As the Führer once said," the tall man concluded, and five further speeches followed. Each successive speech surpassed the stupor of the initial one in its liveliness and effusiveness. The abyss that had allowed itself to be filled up with these speeches opened up and then disappeared, but remained visible in the wide-eyed looks all around, in the similarity of the expressions on their faces. They beamed as they had beamed at that time.

Joseph saw the young priest vanish from the crowd. He would have liked to follow him, but he decided not to. The interplay of language and body, the interplay of the people from the villages whom he knew with the truth that had come over them and emanated from that language compelled him to move even closer to the grave. Gun salutes cracked, the song of the comrade was played, taps blared from the trumpet. The deceased businessman was afforded a grand ceremony, political hope clutched at his death, his departure gave cause to celebrate the presence of that which remained the same, of that which never dies.

After the last speech the rain stopped, the clouds broke up, and a yellow ray of sunlight shot like an arrow across the sky. Herons rose up from the nearby pond and flew off over the cemetery.

As he was leaving, Joseph understood that more had taken place here than the mere continuation of the *Movement* which would die out when death claimed the remaining people present. Joseph sensed the reawakened presence of what recurred continuously. The gathering of the green coats, the hunting-like outfits, the recollection that they appeared in like manner at every possible occasion, above all at church ceremonies, countermanded the impression that this was just a case of personal guilt exerting itself here alongside personal responsibility. The disbanding community of mourners swallowed up the individuals. Over all of them hovered a murmuring whisper they all imitated. They stood in a glow of light and there was nothing in this light that would have been able to drive them from it. As always and forever, they, the pawns of truth, pressed their way here. That the death of the one they honored as a model could have been a departure from this truth, a return of the truth to the earth that encompassed these secrets, yes, who would carry that back into this earth? They were blind to anything that might be accessible outside of their truth. Any desired insight into this madness can only be realized outside of this madness. But the burial had affirmed itself in it. Later on at the funeral banquet they cheerfully celebrated a victory. Once again one of them was left unbrokenly whole. Moving from table to table, those who had slipped out of their gray coats confirmed that the yearly Yule celebrations of this region would continue to imbue the Movement with life. The musicians moved about from one room to the next, they provided accompaniment for the old songs, and right in the midst of it all, Joseph realized that over the course of his entire lifetime things in his country had never been any different. What had been was present, embedded in the now. No part of it could be separated from the whole or sink into oblivion. Attempting to understand it from a particular point in time was also an impossibility. The Movement had shed its claim to a particular time and to specific economic conditions for its justification.

They ate beef with horseradish, the gray banquet of death. The pork roast that followed tempted them to say that they had all been lucky. The wine and the beer fortified the truth. Late in the night Joseph felt boxed in by the deadly phrase we-are-who-we-are. Meanwhile, the men in gray had left, because they had things to take care of elsewhere. Joseph transformed the proximate, well-known faces of classmates and neighbors into a series of pictures ranging from hate to forgiveness. Where would he have had to go to speak of forgiveness without shame? Since the past had remained present for so many, there was no such thing as forgiveness.

It was a splendid, sunny day in Abano. Was there not some inconsistency in seeking out the baths and massages in the chambers and enclosed rooms and not remaining outside in the open air? In these inner rooms the funeral would continue and the purging of truth in vapor and steam would be perhaps more difficult than at other places.

Joseph's body was here, his life up until now, what he had done and must do, what he thought and had to think. The urge to provide relief to the body of his person, so that the pain in the joints disappeared before they made it impossible to keep his experiences intact, gave him the patience for what awaited him. In the dining room in the evening, surrounded by the green tapestries and the oversized mirrors, next to the swinging glass door with the oversized handles, he ate alone at a small table. With each entering guest the belabored effort of walking, the submissive pose of the cure, also arrived.

Abano, place of expurgated pain, the dormant volcanoes contained the movement of their eruption, the hot waters revived the memory, the continuing flow made the beginning appear inexhaustible, lying far ahead of the figures toward which it pushed forward.

In the morning Joseph was awakened and summoned for his initial massage. He passed up breakfast to be one of the first ones in the treatment room. On the way there the desire to depart quickly was already stronger than the acknowledgment that his body needed the treatment. As with many hypochondriacs, Joseph's fears about his own body were diversions from the actual condition of the body, a denial of aging, a miscalculation of time, an overestimation of the present.

The masseuse beckoned Joseph to lie down on the massage table. He did so with a motion of his hand, which had already commanded hordes of people to the table. The wave of the hand did not distinguish among the flow of bodies, the Movement pressed out portions from the mass of those seeking a cure, half bodies, whole bodies, one and a half bodies; it abused the invisible self in the comings and goings of the flesh. Lying on his back, Joseph cringed before his own body, before its whiteness, its flabbiness, its rigidity. The masseuse positioned Joseph's legs, tugged briefly on them and began to knead them, and doled out occasional blows with his tightened palm. The loud slapping sound caused Joseph to squeeze his eyes shut tightly. The body of the deceased businessman surfaced, his presence at gruesome deeds, the places where he had been, the sensually powerful presence when he entered the rooms of his business establishment. He saw the man's corpse lying in the hospital morgue, between the corpses stacked above one another, then on the table. For one last time the one who he had been. More easily describable than ever before.

When Joseph opened his eyes again, he recoiled from the grim look on the masseuse's face, from his square head, the protruding chin, and the short-cropped hair. He would not have been surprised if the man's hands had ripped him open. Joseph was embarrassed about his body in front of him, and had he spoken the man's language, he would have apologized for his body, for his age, for his audacity at even lying here. Joseph knew that the masseuse, who intermittently sang a few bars from Verdi operas, was off in another world as he pondered all sorts of things other than the body beneath his hands. Nevertheless, he was afraid of being in his sight, in the proximity of his body, two bodies that contradicted each other and were not actually where they were, but rather in separate worlds. The masseuse signaled to him with his hand which way he should turn. Shaking his head and clapping his hands, the masseuse became impatient and irritated whenever Joseph failed to position his body correctly. It must have seemed intentional to the masseuse that Joseph never responded correctly the first time. He even confused left and right, at best it took him several seconds before he coordinated turning and direction. "Never been a soldier," the masseuse said as he broke his silence. Joseph did not reply, he remembered one of his instructors who had drilled them during the war at the home, backed up by the director of the home, an SS officer, and who trained them in movement, formations, and endurance.

Right in the middle of this thought, as if he wanted to prevent its welling up into the present, the masseuse rubbed and pressed the palms of his hands over Joseph's back. The slaps on his shoulders that followed caused Joseph to turn on his side and draw up his legs. For a few seconds the masseuse retreated, sang a few snippets of melodies with his deep bass voice, cursed, and, reaching for Joseph again, continued the massage even more mechanically than before. How many bodies must he have had beneath him. What hatred he must have felt for them, hatred of the visible presence of the past, of the scars, blemishes, swollen places, ganglia, knots, of the wretchedness and ugliness, of the herding together of the sufferings and of their hope, of their wish that he could expunge the notion from them that they were broken-down bodies. Angrily the masseuse kneaded his revulsion into the mire of flesh, and Joseph surmised that he probably imagined himself smashing the shell of the boys with a hard one, so that none of them would forget his flesh and his decrepitude. Without warning the masseuse stopped, stepped over to the sink, and washed his hands with green soap. As he was drying his hands, he motioned to Joseph that he could leave the room. Joseph proceeded into the adjacent indoor pool and lay down on the chaise lounge. He draped a white towel over his upper body. He drew up his right leg to support the book he held in his hand. For the first time in quite a while he looked closely at the long scar on his upper thigh, and the scar led him back to the wound, and it seemed to him as if there were nothing to remember but a present full of pieces torn off that spread out incessantly, and each one was simultaneously his past and his future.

Outside a heavy rain had begun to fall. Joseph tried to look at the water running down the large window panes, the drops that flowed into the whole and were lost in it, how they raged and became mighty in the wider streams of water, how accommodatingly the prevailing force of gravity took charge, as a unifying *movement*, as something from the future. And as the life that had carried him along up to that point surprised him image by image, he knew, because the recurrence was like a foreshadowing, that life coming from the future could only be purified there.

1

The headmaster's written evaluation prevented Joseph from taking the entrance examination for the secondary school.

Sunlight etched itself into the welts on his body. Joseph was happy about his father's anger, about his despair; the father is stretched to his limits with the son. Make my dream come true, the dream and the anger, look at the oak trees, listen to the restless quarry, the quail are stirring in the grain fields, they flee, sweeping waves over the fluttering tips of the wheat in the fields.

It's better not to leave the park by a narrow path or through a gap in the thorny hedge. Feel yourself protected by the tree-lined paths. They will help you move on, they will take you in again. Chose a path from whose middle the horizon and the house you are leaving are equidistant. The linden trees give comfort, the red swarm of insects between the backs of the protruding roots writes your story.

The rain from the thunderstorms lashed against the windowpanes. Joseph looked out onto the large field, the stacks of hay shriveled. The wind tore off clumps and scattered them about. It was still quite warm, the smell of horses rose from the stalls extending at a right angle along the long, one-story house and closing off the farmyard, the protected play area to the south. From the farmyard came the shouting of soldiers.

The smashed panes transformed the meadow into a pond. The dams prevented flooding, the herons alighted when the lightning struck. Joseph feared what the sight of them portended. The father had told the son what it meant: white, covetous arrows, death. They hid in the trees, looking like pale bones from the distance. In flight they encircled the victims.

On the previous day the gaunt SS man, holding the other arrow with the fishing tackle in his hand, stood upright, on the landing leading out into the pond. He was angry at the water, the fish, the people. The swimmer floated motionless in the water.

"You aren't allowed to fish here," Joseph calls out.

"Get lost, you farm-boy." The fishing line swished over his head, the boots cracked on the oaken posts.

The thunderstorm subsided, the clouds evaporated, the sun broke through. Joseph tore open the window. Vapor rose from the meadow, the horses pawed at the stable floor, all around the house orders bellowed. He leaned out of the window and took a breath, the leaves of the trees shone brighter than before. Women came to the meadow with rakes and spread out the hay for drying, the diagonal row moved back and forth silently, one after the other they removed their kerchiefs.

He loved the wind in his hair, as it caressed his head softly. What was unknown outside disappeared. It became a secret again. In it the paths were protected. The world moved forward on them, their borders were in every step, a step of darkness, a step of light.

He loved having a clear head but did not trust it. The theses and their opposites alike were what drove out the fear. The tension subsided and released what had been excluded. On the way to the Third, things reversed themselves again.

For three weeks the soldiers had been there. An entire division spread out over a large area. The colonel limped across the square in front of the villa; his monocle had the area in its line of sight. Since the First World War he is said to have a silver plate where his buttocks were. Did the soldiers take Joseph for a fool? He loved storytellers because he didn't have to believe them. Truth existed only so that it be punished. It showed up where the teacher spoke, or when he stood in front of the three fallen German soldiers, next to the suspension bridge to Yugoslavia.

The German soldiers had advanced into Yugoslavia over this bridge. Blood spurted from the jugular vein of the customs official on the other side; the bullet had struck him in his sleep. The news of a quick victory spread like a wildfire through the entire area.

2

People sat in their rooms with maps in front of them, totally immersed in their conversations, in messages, and they seized land and obliterated it. The enthusiasm produced a common mug. Prior to the war they lived discontentedly; their hatred lacked focus. The enemy had not yet been dragged out. Now they understood the meaning of it. Everyone had at least one person around him to watch and to destroy.

3

The women had long since disappeared from the meadow. The evening sun set in a brilliant display; the wind caused it to change in an array of colors. Reaching over his head, his mother had closed the window. His grandfather sat at the edge of the corner bench and held his hand over his heart. The old man's big blue eyes caught sight of him.

"The SS moved out today," his grandfather said. "Thank God. The soldiers are poor devils, the SS are devils." Breathing heavily, the grandfather left the kitchen. "He's old and doesn't understand the times we live in." Later on his mother brought the old man's meal to his room. The smoke from a Virginia cigar wafted through the door.

How he made those camellias bloom! Small and fragile, he puttered in the hothouse, hunched over, with the green watering can in his hand. The hand with the brown spots trimmed the wild growth out of the proliferating branches. The hand had polished silver, served from silver, folded napkins, cleaned coats of arms, wiped his own sweat from his brow. In the old days.

4

Seeking redemption is the bane of the modern day. Hope plagued the day, the one who could offer them fulfillment was active in all of them. Nobody feared this disease. It lay hidden in the health, in the glow, in the meshing wheels. Providence chooses only the One. Everything else is destroyed by the same One. There is no madness, only the continuation of what remains the same. The Sunday of life arrives. He who defends the flag, he who sacrifices his blood: every recruit becomes part of the wider recruitment to the Movement. What is new *is*, and the resulting action flows forth inexhaustibly. Nothing can be changed. Whatever destroys truth and order will be destroyed. That this will come to pass is the hope.

5

Skittishly the horses in the stable paw at the floorboards; their hooves resound on the rounded wood of the stable floor. "A person can't sleep." The father goes to the window and peers out through the crack in the curtains.

"If they hear a plane, they hold me responsible." The uniform lies on the bedroom floor. "Leave it there." The mother considers her good fortune that her husband is in charge of the air-raid unit south of the town. He had been selected for the job. He knew the area; the ponds and forests also needed him.

At home the division's first lieutenant slept, having taken up his quarters there in the room next to the grandfather's. "I hate having to show respect day after day in my own home, in front of you, in front of the children, in front of my furniture, my guns, my clothes, my bread." "Soon the Führer will need them somewhere else," replied the mother.

6

The spaces the birds, the buzzards, the hawks, the pheasant, crows, woodcock, doves, jays, and clouds occupied lost their individual significance to other signs. "The skies are being threatened," said the father. His eyes and ears hurt. Looking and listening and reporting. The cloud cover robbed his eyes of their power. The father was condemned to listen. There was no more peace and quiet, the air was rushing water, the night was inundated. Chaotic stimuli. The sound of the screams, a deciphered sign of life, was a consolation when it struck Joseph, struck itself, struck the teacher, struck the shame. Just because of one sentence from the child-eating demon: "And therefore the student is not a German youth." It was the mouth that roared what *was*.

The weak-hearted grandfather's dry cough echoed through the house, the difficult breathing, the loneliness and the difference between their daily routines and the life and glorified death foisted upon them. What kind of aging would be victorious over this madness?

The mother slept soundly, she was as yet still untroubled by any worry that what was wished for could have been the wrong wish. The father's heavy breathing subsided. "Her breathing is solid like the earth." All of a sudden the first rays of light in the east. Time to go back to bed or to go to the forest. If it were March, he would already be standing at the edge of the upper forest and looking over to the fir trees that had been left standing in groups on the ridge. The slope is brighter in the morning light. He heard the cock among the fir trees. The great expectation of perceiving the outbreak of nature there, the mating song out into the clearing, the desire to set oneself free, to be there in song, immersed in life, to be deaf out of sheer pleasure! The clicking sound of the voice arose; during the first climax, he moves out a few paces in unison with the voice, with his gun in his hand, and waits silently, until the song begins again. He sees the cock's outstretched head and its wings pointed down at an angle; gasping, scratching sounds resound in his direction. The cock hops and dances, he fires into this tumult, and for the moment there is relief from the guilt and shame that had turned his face, his whole body, to stone.

7

Who could have eased the suffering where they lived? In their need the flies that the Devil had them eat were victorious. The hunger was stilled. Now there were words that they spoke with the same voice. One reached beyond his own dwelling, the four walls broke open, the feelings and sensations came from outside and united them with the others, as if they were all in a common procession on the road to salvation.

8

He had struck the son. The son was excluded. He was not admitted, he did not fit the mold of what was demanded of a German secondary-school student. He had thought that now even for someone like him the path would be open. He saw the body of his child.

He lashed the whip.

The son knelt and held his back ready. With every blow his appreciation of his father increased; he sensed his father's suffering. The tall, slender man, whose cheek he had always somewhat feared, whose lips he scarcely dared look at, fused with him in rage. For the first time he struck the *other*, which had seduced him into feeling himself hidden in him. He struck his son, because he was searching for what was foreign, he recaptured his own abyss. He tore away the paths, the tree-lined paths crumbled, father and son presented each other pain and anger, both increased their feeling for the other, "for you my pain, for you my anger." When they were then standing face to face, they were living human beings, and each of them peered endlessly deeper into the other, look for look.

The wounds on the skin, the victories of the rod, afforded the privilege of being consoled. They attracted the grandfather's hand, the healing touch; they unleashed love in the mother's face. The welts signified the return of the family, their dwelling place, the sign for his brother and his sister. The welts circumscribed the family; they created the protection of being different.

9

A few days later the farmyard was empty; the soldiers had withdrawn, the smell of horses was the parting gift, and the tracks in the meadows, which had been made by the horses' hooves and the wheels. The departure hurt. It was as if that which had always been there left, one thing after the other. "Has the Reich abandoned us already?" asked the grandfather. On June 22, 1941, the hour of death commenced for the departed soldiers. Other than those soldiers spotting aircraft, the father was now the only soldier in the village.

By this time Joseph's wounds were already covered with crusty scabs that began peeling off. A letter arrived. The uncle had accomplished it with his influence, "with his music," the beaming father said. Joseph would be allowed to take the entrance exam in the fall. If he passed it, he would be monitored until the end of the year, and then the blemish on his school record would be forgotten.

When Joseph went to get the wine to celebrate, he saw a crack in the damp blackish brown earth in front of the vat in the cellar. A red salamander was running along it. He tapped on the vat and could tell that it was almost empty. The wine had seeped off into the crack, had been swallowed up, stolen. Joseph followed the crack that ran before him, over the four stone steps, across the farmyard to the wooden steps, up to the second story and under the table at which his father was sitting and twirling the empty wineglass impatiently in his hands. The father drank the wine with lips protruding and smacked them after each swallow. The words on his tongue placated his eyes, the crack divided itself in them into two paths that crossed and disappeared.

A knock at the door transformed the room. The credenza, stove, wood box, and sink tore themselves from the table at which the father and the son were sitting. The mother moved away from the stove and positioned herself by the window, as if she were looking for a way out, his brother and sister ran out through a second door into the adjoining room.

After the second knock that was much softer, indeed, almost solicitous, the father responded, "Come in." Only when the man was standing in the middle of the kitchen, did the mother say: "Oh, it's you." "Pardon me for coming to see you in my officer's uniform," said the mother's cousin from the neighboring village. "I've just arrived from Yugoslavia, for a few days, I'll be going back right away to the city, to my wife Molly."

Only when the grandfather came through the door and the officer said, "Hello, Uncle," did the father stand up and offer his hand.

Joseph had to go get more wine. He brought it into the hunting room. Joseph saw tears in his uncle's eyes.

The afternoon sun beat down. The shadow from the clump of linden trees in the yard was not expansive enough to douse the heat. Joseph's brother and sister stood fixated next to him and observed how he hovered over the little sulfur flame and breathed in the smoke. With the taste of blood in his mouth he rolled over in front of the bench, on which the sulfur was burning in a hole.

Coughing he said: "I'm remembering things, I'm remembering things, because I have to leave."

Since the uncle's visit the family concealed a secret. "The opposite side of the medal," said the father. "I have to believe it if he said it," the mother added.

After the war they recounted what they had heard from the uncle. He had already died as a prisoner of war, his son had been killed, and his wife Molly had been forced from her apartment and moved to a different one.

10

The heron had arisen to reveal the Order, the new course, the assault. "Learn from the pain," the father said. The heavens awaited the planes, the eyes burned from looking, the points on the compass stiffened. During the military occupation of Yugoslavia the uncle served in a unit which was to maintain the Order. Joining the weapons was the weapon of truth, the recompense for all time. He had broken off his theology studies after the First World War because of his wife, and he regained the respect of the scandalized family and the parish community only when he became a police officer, and in this way wended his way back into the Order. From there he was summoned to the military police. It was a punishment, he stated on that afternoon. He had been condemned, commanded to be present at executions, condemned to gaze into hell. He had been dragged into horror. In the beginning they were received amicably, but the ulcers had been removed. He was turned to stone, which had to be what it was. It was impossible for him *not* to be what he was condemned to be. Fascism is something that tolerates nothing but itself, it kills for the present, for the unadulterated, which is either truth or rubble and ashes. "The fact that the officers cry gives me hope," said the grandfather.

11

The tears amidst the overwhelming power of the present from which no one can remove himself were traces of what was missing in the present, as if one heard a silent voice, as if there were light only in the darkest night, as if the truth were suffocating beneath the veil. Joseph left the farm. "I am always here and can only be so if I leave." He gazed onto the pond, onto the wide flat expanse overgrown with green. Names for the plants, insects, and birds swirled in his head. He was hardly able to arrange any of them in order. He had heard them from the people, from his father, from the people guarding the pond. What appeared and the names for them he kept separate, he took the names home with him as his toys. What they connoted was no longer the ponds and insects and plants. Through them he became more intimate with the world, because they were foreign to him, because every leaf surpassed the glance and already belonged to the other. He continued walking along a row of alders and then upon a group of elm trees to the old oaks. At the edge of the park grew the tall acacias, and here and there elderberry ran wild. He followed the old paths and soon arrived where he liked being best, on the path lined with linden trees. It stretched out from the park into the fields. In front of the cross at the end of the path he stopped at the place where his parents had taken his picture every year since his third birthday. At this spot the earth did not turn, it was the center of life for everything later on.

Farther inside, where the park became an overgrown forest, he came upon a swarm of gnats, which, attracted by the smell of his skin, continued to followed him. He flailed into their dance with a branch he had snapped off. But the swarm continued to encircle him, as if he were under water. Only at a clearing that was heavily covered with moss did the gnats set him free. At this spot a turning point had once occurred, his body became a body. The body withdrew into the body, he felt ashamed. Joseph stared and saw the other bodies. They had pulled down their pants and were sitting on the ground with their legs spread wide and stroking their genitals with one hand. They were the bodies of children after their First Holy Communion. One of the boys brought him to the group. "Do it, too," he said, and because it did not work, he looked upon the others as higher creatures.

Father and mother then stood more distant in the evening. He withdrew from his father, because he could not stand his smell. His mother's eyes became puzzled. Only the grandfather had nothing to do with what he had experienced. He remained soft like his flowers.

He left the clearing and came to a path, on which the tracks of horses and the imprint of soldiers' boots could still be seen. They had survived. In the branches the acorn jays hopped and ascended and descended as they flew away. Joseph ran across the large meadow. On it his father had first set foot upon this place, where he had now been for years, silent in his desire beneath the rule of an image which his father had given him the command to live.

12

Joseph knew from his headmaster that he did not conform to the new image. In comparison to it he stood as the one cast outside of the mold. Against the backdrop of this image his father had struck him, and since then he shied away from the image. The rods tamed the image, the physical pain freed the body, his sight, his senses. They loved the father, loved his pain, the unsettled gait, the wrinkles in his forehead. His angry voice aroused gentleness. The mother joined in. She tore off a piece of the urgency and transformed it into a material that resisted the urgency. She destroyed the burden. She did not work, she spread happiness. Where there was so little, where the rooms were cramped and the means meager and all around eyes threatened, to whose firm gaze she was subjected, there she enriched the family and bestowed upon it the feeling of *who* they were. However, the stream into which the parents had entered, on which they let themselves be carried, rose into the partially cloudy sky across the meadow and turned there in a circle, in a whirl, which threatened to sweep the parents along with it. Joseph continued on to the dock by the pond on which the SS soldier had been standing straight with his fishing pole, with his face as well as his nose drawn long. His neck was thin and sunken in the back so that the sinews disappeared like ropes from his head down into his body.

On the pond the water-bugs darted, they hardly left a trace behind on the grayish green film of algae covering the surface. Around the dock the water lay in the shadow of the large plane trees. When the wind stirred its leaves, shafts of light illuminated the water's surface and shone so harshly that they swallowed up the skittering water-bugs.

In the middle of the pond the white water lilies glistened among dark green leaves. Ducks were swimming at the edge and looked up whenever a fish jumped. In the pond was a small island built long ago. It, as well as the glistening flowers the grandfather had planted, could be reached by an arched bridge.

A small road passed by the pond and connected the closely grouped houses in the park with the village to the west. On the field in front of it stood the air-raid station. On this road the son encountered the father, as he was coming home from duty on his bike. The wheels of the bike made a crunching sound on the fine pebbles. The sound became louder because the father slowed down as soon as he saw Joseph. He moved the handlebars back and forth trying to keep his balance. Joseph stopped, neither said a word, neither looked into the other's eyes, as if they were ashamed at having met one another, as if they had looked through one another or had something to hide from the other. They were too close to one another, each feared discovering some warning sign in the other. Joseph saw himself as the father, the father saw himself as the son. Only when Joseph no longer heard the crunching sound from the bike did he turn around and look after the father, until he disappeared behind a hedge of lilac. It was easy to imagine himself riding off on the bike, as if the father had taken along his ego, which the headmaster had advised him to fortify.

13

All summer long no soldiers came to the area. And therefore the news about those soldiers who had died came all the more unexpectedly. The optimistic messages from the outset turned somber. The prophet sought new, fresh voices in order to strengthen his own voice; he kept an eye out for helpers' helpers, for willing blood. His world was not to become a fable. Reality needed to be attended to, experiences that themselves told this reality, with the witnesses of its truth.

The helpers arrived in brown uniforms. The straps, medals, and boots glistened in the August sun; they were not unfamiliar. Before the war they were people like everyone else, discontent behind the graves and fences of their need, their possessions, or their lack of possessions. Now they were in charge, walked past the churchgoers, made jokes about the way Jews looked. "She has miserably crooked legs like a Jew." They guarded assemblies, traveled throughout the countryside with collection boxes, drew up lists, gathered signatures. They forced their way into the cash boxes, collected furs, sought support for the front, controlled waste, peeked into pots, counted cows and pigs, observed how people greeted each other, collected the contributions, ordered the picking of medicinal herbs, inspected the books, joined in the festivities, in the celebrations and the gatherings. They suppressed the voices of opposition. The headmaster, who wanted all of them to act as *one* person, was in charge.

Joseph recalled the time when he got to know the people among whom he was now living.

They emerged out of the fog. No spark came from their faces. They were shut off, as if damned to be only themselves. They lived in the villages, sometimes alone in far-off corners of the forest, out of the way. They were together at mass, at burials, for hunts. Each one kneeled down differently from the other, each one threw the shovel of dirt onto the grave differently, each one had a different way of raising his rifle and firing it. Only in the inns did a trace of similarity reside in their faces, although they, precisely when they were drunk, distanced themselves most fundamentally from one another, yes, were even creative in protecting their personal brand of terror and underhandedness.

Now it was even difficult for Joseph to distinguish among the people of the surrounding area. Their faces were muted. They retreated into uniformity and looked like one egg among other eggs.

From their mouths Joseph heard the talk of German blood; he heard them speak of profundity, of bondedness, of that which was unattainable by the enemy.

It sounded as if they were not talking about themselves, as if they had forgotten who they were, as if they were trying to deceive themselves. They were not conscious of the fact that they had changed, or that they had totally lost *their* consciousness, the boundaries of their place. They let themselves overflow their banks and sweep over into one another. After the hunt, standing in front of their quarry, they were as indistinguishable from one another as rabbits with gray fur.

"Joseph, you're not going to have it easy," said his father. "You are being drawn away from the community. You are looking for the immutable, you like something only when it has a flaw, if others do not possess it in the same way. You are happy when a mushroom grows a deformed double cap, when the trees are gnarled, when the fruit trees are covered with mistletoe and die off from it. From among a hundred fish you snatch the one fish with the deformed fin. You walk behind the stunted person and peer through the windows in order to see the deformed people squatting on their stools. You listen up when the hens crow, you run off with the children to the place where two male dogs are mating. You tore out the photograph of a hermaphrodite from Grandfather's book, and how often have we had to force you to come home because you could not tear yourself away from the crazy woman in the village. You were happy when you got a beating."

14

The large rectangular farm building outside of the park had housed displaced Poles for over a year. The headmaster forbade the children from going near the Poles or from greeting them when they encountered them. Joseph's father was in charge of the work detail with the Poles. He was afraid because it was impossible for him to treat the Poles any differently than the locals. The women worked in the fields, the men in the forest. One woman, with whom Joseph met secretly because she had such wonderful stories to tell, was a cook in the farm kitchen. He brought her books from the library of his other grandfather, who lived nearby in a vintner's cottage and whom people called the philosopher. Joseph pilfered decorative Reclam volumes from him. "Oh, Kant," said Maria Szmaragovska, "oh, Schopenhauer, oh, Nietzsche," and Joseph kept it his secret that she knew the names on his grandfather's books. Maria Szmaragovska was tall and thin, her hair was dark and cut short. She had radiant eyes. She always carried one of the books hidden beneath her clothing. Often she could not take it out of the sewn-in pocket for days. "It's good that you are here," she said to Joseph. "You make it easier for me to be in *this* part of the world. When I see you, I know that this strange world belongs to everyone."

Totally separated from the Poles and other inhabitants of the farm building, French prisoners of war lived behind barred windows in several rooms on the second floor. They had arrived a few days after the German soldiers had been deployed to Russia. The day of their arrival was a noteworthy one for Joseph. It brought what for him had previously hardly been imaginable: *the enemy soldier*, the defeated, imprisoned enemy, the one about whom he had been hearing every day since the beginning of the war, who was present but invisible. Now he was here in the flesh in his tattered clothing, with his sack across his shoulder, with his cloddy shoes and his battered cap. With an uncertain glance the prisoners stared at the men in the brown uniforms and looked towards the prison guards, as if they hoped the guards would protect them from those with the shiny boots and the brown uniforms.

Roger Vergely was the name of one of the Frenchmen. After a heavy thunderstorm, water had seeped into the cellar of Joseph's parents' home. Vergely waded into it with rubber boots and laboriously scooped out the water that had seeped into the cellar, bucket by bucket.

Joseph followed the laborious comings and goings of the man through the cellar window; he was incapable of carrying out the work assigned to him. He saw the defeat of a human being, and it jolted him from his silent watch. He ran to his father and found no words for the soldier's pain. He took his father by the hand and led him to the cellar window.

The next day Roger Vergely sat in the long hall outside the rooms where they lived.

Before him was an easel. He was painting the farm, as seen from the hallway. Joseph followed the picture through its developing stages, and saw how it changed the farm. His father had found out from Roger Vergely that he was a painter—"also an incomplete human being," said his father, because he himself had also sat occasionally in front of the easel. He put Vergely in his place in their home.

A few days later his father sent the painter into the living room. People had asked his father who that was who observed the surroundings from the windows. If it was a captured Frenchman, then he had no right to be looking at our homeland so unrestrictedly. They warned the father of his evil look. The mother, more cautious than the father, closed the living room jalousies and opened the door from the bedroom to the hallway. Thus the natural light and a partial view were maintained. The grandfather brought cigarettes, the mother invited Vergely for dinner. There was a guest in the house. He shifted the boundaries. The grandfather breathed more freely, he brought home flowers and placed them in the living room. "If they deny him the world, he should have it inside, we won't let the world pass by."

Several of his father's friends who had seen the paintings had said at the time that the Frenchman was crazy. He had left out of his pictures what was most evident, something the headmaster had brought into order in the art classes within the drawn boundaries of the sketchbook. The Frenchman had bad eyes.

In Vergely's pictures other eyes opened and closed, the pictures belonged to them. Other colors radiated. The beloved trees and facades, to which the colors clung, pointed beyond themselves. What Joseph had learned to see at that time in his parents' living room led him beyond the familiar threshold. His mother stood at the window and looked into the red glow of the evening, his grandfather took Joseph's hand and raised it up in front of the chalice-shaped blossoms. "Retract your claws so that they take hold of you."

His mother hid Vergely's paintings in the wash basket beneath the uniform that his father had received. His father had just been discharged from military duty, because he was indispensable in a war industry. Instead of searching for planes in the sky, he was now looking in Vergely's paintings for the foreign for which, as a soldier, he had had to ferret out in the skies.

During the night the Frenchmen were moved out. Vergely left behind a painting which consisted of only one color, a bright green. The emptiness was filled with this green, and the green also danced in them as a reminder that they had not avoided the encounter with the enemy. They had gone beyond the forbidden, unintentionally, almost against their will. A hidden power had gone to the extreme, to the foreign, to the exciting feeling, within their small dwelling, in which it was also said there is only one Führer and one Volk.

Since that time the mother allowed the grandfather to remove the maps of the battle sites from the kitchen and to stow them away in the attic. It was actually the attic with its corners and little cubbyholes that gained in importance. Still without apparent reason, they sat together and discussed where the good hiding places were; the father nailed together crates and lined them with tin. One could bury the most important things in them. Nevertheless, they still believed in victory.

15

But they did not talk about what would come after the victory. For Joseph nothing was darker than the future, even though all he heard about from people and in school was about this future. There were farmers in the village who talked about resettlements and fantasized about the future.

They were available for the eastern regions, and those in charge also knew who of them might settle in the East. Joseph had heard talk about it in his father's hunting room. He observed his mother's wide open eyes and his father's mechanical nodding of his head.

When they were alone again, they said almost simultaneously: "But we are staying, we are staying here." They needed this landscape, the song, the birds, the simultaneity of the thick flowing green, in which the power to flee and gravity coalesced.

16

Joseph met Maria Szmaragovska as he was walking around the perimeter of the park between the oaks and hazel bushes, looking for strawberries, observing the jays, listening to the hollow sounds of the pigeons as they alighted. She led him from tree to tree, from flower to flower, and labeled them with the names of her language. He said to her: "I have never been as close at home as here." "You can't pop your eyeballs out of your head," replied Maria Szmaragovska. "You can no longer see the way you once did. If you are in the city and they tell you about its splendors and important things, keep yourself out of it. You and your domain, I know, are inseparable."

17

The summer came to an end. Joseph had to study every day for several hours. He sat in his grandfather's room, the blinds were half drawn, flies were circling around in the room, and lighted on the fringe of the ceiling light or crawled into the vase of flowers. Outside the late summer was filled with warmth. Joseph spent his free time with other children. He convinced them to go with him to the stables, to roam through the village, to look for fish in the streams. They climbed in the haylofts, buried themselves in the fresh hay, they passed unnoticed over the roofs, sneaked into yards at evening, eavesdropped on people through windows, they shooed the wild ducks, threw stones at dogs and cats, and when they were in the vicinity of the air-raid station, they hid and held hands because it was war, about which they had still seen little. When the first soldier from the village was killed in battle, they avoided the family's house as if the horror might overcome them.

At the end of August Joseph boarded the train with his parents and traveled with them to the city. It was the second time that he had been there.

When they got off the train, there were hundreds of Hitler cub scouts standing at the train station grouped in formations. In front of each of the groups, the *individual ones*, who stand in front of groups, stood tall. Joseph was startled, because he was wearing the same white socks as this sea of legs. Joseph and his parents walked along the wall of the train station building to the streetcar. He knew that he should have already joined the Hitler Youth a half year ago. They hadn't taken him yet because he would be signed up in the fall in the city anyway. Father and mother were silent. Joseph latched on tightly to the seat in the streetcar. Flags lined the streets, shop after shop, house door after house door. People and houses seemed to him to be squeezed together. There were a lot of soldiers among the pedestrians. His father explained the uniforms to him. As they were waiting at an intersection, his father pointed out a two-story building to him. Mighty columns set into the wall flanked the entrance. The windows were closed and dusty. A wide flag with a swastika waved over the entrance. "This is the high school," his father said, "but not yours."

First they visited Aunt Molly. Annoyed, she related that his uncle had tried to get transferred. The unit behind the front had become unbearable, he had said. He wanted to join a fighting unit. But she had talked him out of it in front of Hitler's picture and made it clear to him that the most urgent matter was to educate the conquered territories in our spirit, she said. They did not budge from their seats in the small kitchen; they were not allowed in the living room, because it had been straightened up *forever*. Rooms also exist to allow the Order to become visible. Where one lives is the best place. Then she led them all into the bedroom. At the foot of the double bed was a green sofa. "Here you will sleep well and above all on time," she said to Joseph. He nodded as he stared at the picture of his uncle with his son, who was also an officer; it stood on the piano in the sealed-off living room. The collar of Joseph's coat began rubbing against his neck. The discomfort continued as they made their way to the school, where Joseph and his parents had to introduce themselves to the principal.

The school, a three-story complex consisting of several buildings, was nondescript. The dirty green blinds were partially closed. The entrance into the building that formed the one street corner was situated in a small side street, a dead-end, that led to a church.

A narrow staircase brought them to the second floor. The superintendent, a small crippled man with a large hump, whose body moved like a sickle as he walked, led them to the principal's office. He knocked and, after the reply to enter, he opened the door as he turned around. On the brown lapel of his coat was the Party insignia. Behind the rimless glasses lay ominous eyes. With his especially long arms, one of which extended to his knee, he pushed Joseph into the principal's office. The principal was friendly, said they would give Joseph a chance, that he had until the end of the year, which was also the end of the trimester, to prove himself. Only at that point did Joseph notice that his father was also wearing the Party insignia, which again disappeared when they left the school.

They visited his father's brother for an hour, the one who had facilitated Joseph's conditional acceptance. The uncle was sitting at the piano in the parlor when they entered. Joseph walked over to the uncle, who extended his hand to him after a while. His father and mother had stayed standing in the doorway. The uncle got up; then they sat down at the large dining table in the middle of the room. Joseph thought about the hunchbacked superintendent, about his distorted face, about the gigantic growth of his hump, as if the SS man from the pond dock had become crippled. He felt the pudgy fingers of the headmaster. With them he smilingly moved along his apparently crooked spine, and the boys and girls had laughed along, because he, a German headmaster, wanted to become more with this spine than they. And even the school guard wore the Party insignia and had a very stern face and calm eyes.

They radiated what they showed; there was nothing hidden behind them, there was nothing beyond them, they stood for that which should be; everything appeared complete.

Joseph walked over to the window and looked down onto the intersection. The streetcar stopped in front of the house door. Sparks flew, as it drove off. The corner houses pointed like arrows towards one another, their imperial facades were well preserved, the many details of their design confused Joseph. The little flags next to the windows fluttered, but dispensed with the harmlessness of the game; they pointed to the deadly seriousness with the ruthlessness of the unambiguous signs. "You can't hide in the city, Joseph," his uncle said suddenly behind his back. "You have to let yourself be seen and see what is necessary." "Otherwise things will go for you like for the wood-grouse," his father added.

When Joseph was sitting at the table again, his mother ran her hand through his hair; she stroked the hair from his forehead, which Aunt Molly had pasted down with her saliva-moistened hand before they left.

Joseph sensed that his mother was protecting him from the aunt and that her enthusiasm for what was new was waning. She was retreating into *her* life.

On the large staircase that led away from the uncle's apartment, Joseph ran ahead with such a burst of energy through the turn of the stairs, that he slipped on the marble floor and fell. He got up and looked at his parents. They did not say a word, but his mother's eyes were opened more widely than normal.

Joseph sat at the window in the train and pressed his forehead against the glass. Five soldiers entered the compartment. Even though they were wearing German uniforms, they did not speak German. Joseph stuck his hands deep into his pants pockets and made fists. One soldier stood up, pushed back Joseph's head without a word, and opened the window half way. Joseph leaned back and continued staring out the window. He would not let himself be deterred from his first journey home. The late afternoon sun shone. Joseph took his hands out of his pockets and rested them on his head and remained sitting this way until they transferred to another train.

The second train traveled back several hundred meters along the same stretch that they had come. Joseph jumped up, but his mother explained to him that the train would soon turn off and then it would just be two more stops and they would be home. Joseph edged closer to his mother. He touched her hand and felt the ring with the stone. He loved the amethyst because his mother had told him that it was the lucky stone for his astrological sign.

A horse and wagon picked them up and took them home. In the yard at the house a group of people awaited them. Among them was Maria Szmaragovska, next to her his grandfather. She was pale as a ghost. When his father climbed down from the wagon, she came forward amidst the deadly silence and pushed the people standing next to her aside to do so. She crossed over the sparse lawn and walked up to the father. Only after she reached the father did her numbness subside.

She began a sentence in Polish but then immediately said in German, "They shot two of us." Joseph jumped from the wagon and stood next to Maria Szmaragovska so that it looked as if he were leaning against her. "Served them right," several people cried out, "they don't want to work since the captured English prisoners arrived and started handing out chocolate, as if they're paying a visit."

The father said quickly: "Come into the office." He left the yard with her. Joseph ran after his mother, who had hurriedly gone up the stairway into the house. With lips blue and hands shaking, his grandfather entered the kitchen visibly upset. He himself had been threatened, as before, when he had stood in a row at the end of the First World War, out of which every fifth person had been shot, because a few people had mutinied against the Kaiser. A farmer had told some SS men, who were drinking beer in the village inn that the Poles thought of themselves as lords, and that they were as haughty as the Jews. Two SS men then grabbed two Poles and the dark-haired cook and interrogated them. They had found a book on her and accused her of theft. The SS men, who were already drunk, had ordered the three Poles to dig a hole in the middle of the village square. He had sat in the inn playing cards and had begun to stand up for the Poles.

"I need them for the gardening," he shouted, "I have to provide war-essential operations." What was supposed to become of the vegetables and the flowers? One of the SS men looked at the book that they had taken from Maria Szmaragovska, and after the three were kneeling in the hole they had dug, they spared Maria Szmaragovska. The SS man had helped her out of the grave.

18

Joseph left the kitchen. He went and got one of Vergely's paintings and stared at it: linden trees filled with leaves covered dark roofs, furrowed strands of clouds moved over the ridges, the folds in the heart of the grandfather, who had the power to tear apart the folds, to let the pain become audible. But the pain was not a voice in the heavens that could be heard. Was it still worth the effort to have it in its place? "This is not for the children," the father said when he came home.

Joseph visited Maria Szmaragovska the next day. She took him to the British prisoners of war, who were lying in the bunk beds dressed in brown uniforms. Large hats were hanging on the beds. There were almost exclusively New Zealanders. One of them gave Joseph several bars of chocolate. Joseph tucked them away in his summer jacket. "The Russians will soon be lying here," said Maria Szmaragovska, "and then others, more and more foreigners will come, and your men will die."

She did not say a word about the murders the day before. She took Joseph along into the kitchen. He stood next to her at the stove. "Cooking dissolves one order and temporarily creates another one, but you can only taste it and smell it," Maria Szmaragovska stated. "Look in this big pot. That's chaos stewing. The bubbles and foam are not running away from order, from unity."

"I'm joining a unit in the city," Joseph interrupted her.

"Then look deeper into the pot. Here chaos is brought to unity, here the abyss opens up, from there it's like being outside in nature, about which you like so much to tell me, where the revelations astonish you and resist your search for names. When you're finally finished with your schooling and if I am still alive, I'll tell you the fairy tale about becoming human."

19

In the evening Joseph's father took him along to the deer blind. Following his father's steps to avoid making sounds as he did, looking along with him, observing him, whether he discovered the deer, and hoping to see it sooner than his father, comprised his actions as he tagged along. Joseph learned to wait. It transformed the ground into something that floated, into which moss and root had apparently interwoven to provide sure footing. What was believed with difficulty and what was certain became a shadow, the shadow of the father and his proximity.

This feeling increased more even when the father climbed onto the high seat with Joseph and their feet swayed between ladder and seat in the void and the seat swayed in the wind. The sacred peace about which his father whispered, the ability for him to breathe more freely there, aroused a certain anxiety in Joseph. The call of birds frightened him, sounds turned to puzzles. Discontentedly Joseph looked down on the barrenness, onto small fir trees, man-high birches and oaks. The deer would have been a redeeming god, but he did not appear.

On the way home Joseph had to walk next to his father. The starry sky was clear and pure. Shooting stars divided up the heavens. Layers of fog were rising over the meadow between the rows of alder; the individual oak trees made the sky shine even brighter. The grass was wet with dew. They crossed a narrow path, the bed of the stream had been dug deeply, the bank broken up here and there. The branches of the weeping willows hung down unevenly. Before the path from the meadow joined the street, Joseph's father stopped and said to him: "Let's protect ourselves, let's protect ourselves. You'll make it, you're weak enough."

During the night Joseph remembered that he had told Maria Szmaragovska about his injuries and the beatings by his father and that he had done it with a bad conscience. It was an attempt to tell her that, but she said only: "There was chaos on your skin. You have opposed the Order that your father is afraid of. What your father is suffering you are supposed to learn not to suffer under. Your father is still the most reachable of what is unreachable. His powerlessness should strengthen you against the powers. Repeat what I say, even if you still don't understand it." Her words brought him no consolation, they gave him the courage for disorder. They penetrated his perception, pushed it forward into what revealed itself. In the face of it he gladly kept silent.

For most of the last day before the separation Joseph wanted to be alone.

It was suddenly impossible for him to show his parents love. His grandfather he spared. He tormented his little sister, he forced his brother to do things that were repulsive to him. While the other children ran along behind the soldiers who passed through the village day after day, he embarked on his secret hikes.

20

In the house with the prisoners of war lived an old chairman of the rural district council, a beer drinker whom hardly anyone had ever seen sober in the afternoon. Nevertheless, he was a welcome visitor at the nearby market and with its academics, doctors, and lawyers. As a student he had belonged to a dueling fraternity, had bumpy scars on his face, and was always ready to shout out who was responsible for the misfortune of the Germans. His friend was a mill master who indulged in research on race theory, collected obscure books on the subject, and with his personal invectives dealt with the separation of the races in his hometown. The chairman had his own conception of paradise; he imagined it being a continuation of the pleasure of that first slug of beer. During his youth he had often been in Bayreuth and knew Cosima Wagner personally. People believed him because he whistled and sang melodies from Wagner. When he was drunk he called himself Amfortas, even though he had no association with Christianity. A disease in the lower part of the body had deprived him of his sexual powers early in life. Naturally women were responsible for his disease, Jews to whom he had wanted to show it. When women passed by in the village or at the market, or when he went by the castle of the neighboring village, in which the working mares lived who saw to the harvesting, he shouted loudly that they were Klingsor's wives. The role National Socialism gave to women was the only thing he did not like about National Socialism. "We're going to go to pot like me because of them," he proclaimed in the inns. Even though he was issued a citation several times by the headmaster because of it, he did not relent from continuing to maintain this belief. Joseph had been afraid of him as a young child, because the chairman's clothes smelled of sweat and he liked to grab him. Now it bothered him so much that he became indignant about living in a building in which Polish rabble and prisoners were housed. He had hated the French and called the British plutocrats who were responsible for the downfall of the Occident, to which only Hitler could put a stop. He much preferred the untamed Russians; it was easier to exterminate the masses than the individualists.

Joseph, the "future academic" and "a hope for the eternal Reich," visited him now because the chairman had invited him several days earlier. Joseph met him at the barber's at the market. Joseph sat next to a five-year-old boy who had come for a German haircut with his grandfather, a veterinarian and one of the chairman's best friends. Joseph saw that the young boy was masturbating under the white drape. Joseph was shocked, above all at his eyes, which he continued to observe in the mirror. The eyes stared straight ahead, but the mouth was poised to laugh. Joseph was afraid someone might notice what was happening. He felt sorry for the grandfather, for everyone in the room, especially for the girl who would be cutting the boy's hair.

Relieved, Joseph left the shop, as if no one else had observed what he had seen. He wanted to get on his bike and ride home on his favorite path alongside the fields, past the ponds, and across the meadows. Suddenly the chairman was standing behind him and said: "Come see me tomorrow, I also saw what the boy did."

Joseph agreed, jumped on his bike, and rode home. The wind striking the skin on his head felt cooler than that against the rest of his body. On his father's recommendation he had had his hair cut very short, so short that it would be impossible for his aunt to insist that it be parted to his forehead. The next day after writing class he went up to see the chairman on the second floor. The chairman approached Joseph with a needle. "I used this to treat myself against the tripper," he said to Joseph. "You know the name for what the boy did yesterday?" "No."

Then the chairman sat down at the table, on which there were several opened, half-empty beer bottles. Joseph had to sit down across from him. "You boys are engaging in masturbation. Didn't your father tell you that that will get into your back?"

Whenever he drank from the bottle, he thrust his head way back. His dirty neck stuck out from the checkered shirt. "We Germans have to multiply, we need children for the whole world. But our enemy is lust. Because we all have this lust, even the other races, it divides us Germans. Lust weakens duty. Lust leads to chaos. Do you know what chaos is? The Führer has rejected lust; therefore, we Germans are the first, and have unity and order. Just look at the rabble that lives in this house, worst of all is the Polish woman. And they give me the food that she cooks."

As he reached for Joseph's hand, Joseph jumped up and ran to the door. "Did you hear me?" the chairman yelled and looked at him with distant eyes. The scars on his face were darker than before. "Look for the goose, you gander," Joseph heard the councilor shout. Then bottles crashed. On the way home Joseph ran into the headmaster. He knew that much now depended on his self-assuredness. "So you want to try it," the headmaster said, "but you always have your hand in front of your fly when you speak to me," droned the headmaster. "Heil Hitler."

21

"To live in seclusion, Joseph, and nevertheless to be a flower," was what his grandfather advised. To be *out there* in seclusion with him, with his mother, with his father, with his brother and sister. No matter where he landed, he would not take them along as pictures and memories. Physically he would be with them, even with the Poles who were shot and the SS man on the pier at the pond. He would meet them everywhere as long as they belonged to the world that had brought them together and that remained part of them.

When the SS men fired at the Poles, an old woman screamed: "Did you hear that, what is that, who's screaming like that? Those can't be people." There is no memory of that, no picture either.

22

Joseph visited the large fir tree in the park. Its trunk vaulted up to the first branches on the side that faced the street. At a height of about three feet, at the deepest point of the indentation, the tree had a circular hole surrounded by a protruding edge. He had often urinated into this hole. He was afraid of the opening and of the green moss around it. The hole also extended down to the inside, a void that he did not fill, that one—so he thought—wanted to rob from him. "It needs to be filled in," threatened the headmaster. The fir tree aroused desire and terror.

The children loved to torment animals. They caught frogs in the pond and peeled off their skin with a pointed wire and enjoyed seeing them resurface again after throwing them in the pond as they stood out from the shimmering surface in their whiteness. They threw mice in wooden containers and, when they reached the edge, pushed them down again into the middle until they drowned. They cut off the wings of birds, watched slaughterings, poured schnapps into the feed of chicken and ducks, and ran about mimicking the wildly fluttering animals. They killed cats. Because the men were not present in many of the homes, they slaughtered the rabbits and the fowl. They found hardly anything for which they needed love, they wanted to be brave, and Joseph consorted with them because he wanted to learn bravery. Many sought the greatness they were told about, but they were only secure in the world of their parents, in the marching orders, at the victory reportings, at the victories of their fathers. They sought a reality without a hole.

23

On the two last days before the entrance examination Joseph reveled in the leisure. The urge for repetition compelled him to his special places.

At the places where the animals were sacrificed he looked for remaining traces. He placed the skin of a frog that he found on the fully opened blossom of a bellflower in a folded handkerchief. Several times he stood before the fir tree. Into it he saw his path continuing, taking leave and returning through the opening. In it his absence should reside. He planted a small, distorted fir tree with bristly protruding branches in front of the large fir tree. It was supposed to hide and protect and preserve the hole.

He spent several hours with his grandfather, whose oft-repeated sentence, "There weren't any such things in my day," comforted him, because what he heard in it was that the future could be different from the bitter present. That his grandfather stood apart from the *Movement*, that his father and mother were now allowing him to do almost anything, he revered as the victory of his grandfather, of that other time, and of tales of that world. His grandfather was the only one whose language was devoid of pride and spite, of slogans of certainty and of truth, Joseph thought. He believed him when he said the world was a garden.

His grandfather often spoke of dying and departing. His difficulty breathing accentuated the leave-taking; it lay on his blue lips. The deep indentations behind his ears were full of it, and whenever his grandfather took out his pocket watch with the handmade gold chain and the two medallions from his vest, it was as if it were the last time. "Getting old redeems time, it brings the future closer. It removes itself from those present decisive faces, it unmasks death's defiance, which disguises death itself as the killing of the enemy. Becoming old vanquishes the compulsion to remain the same, to be always there, to be that which glares out from the calendars, placards, and from the illustrated books." At the chairman's Joseph had thumbed through his book *The Eternal Jew* and through the book of photographs with the beautiful Nordic faces lying next to it. These claims of being genuine faces were negated in the face of the grandfather, it destroyed what was definitive. It radiated and was for Joseph the gateway through which he could continue forth.

24

As Joseph was paging through his ancestral record book that he was supposed to take along to the city, it grieved him that he could only trace his forefathers back to his great-great-grandparents. He would have gladly had the growing number of ancestors, the increase in deaths, the prior dying off as an aggregate of the names there before him. On the other hand, he was happy that they remained hidden from him. The phrase about blood purity had not burned itself into his heart and brain as it had with the others. The Führer's words to the national community aroused his revulsion. To call it fortune to possess pure blood increased his defenses against blood, against the accident of being pure. Having different blood would have meant death. A grandfather with different blood would have been taken from him.

Once again he accompanied his mother to the vegetable garden. Maria Szmaragovska helped her harvest the vegetables. Joseph sat on the sawhorses at the sawmill located next to the garden. He watched the workers and prisoners of war dragging over the tree trunks. The mill foreman's wife was standing in front of the portable circular saw and cut the smaller pieces of wood into kindling. Joseph's father walked between the sawhorses with his yardstick. The sound of the mill could be heard in the distance, the changing sound whenever a trunk was being cut blended with the back and forth singing noise from the circular saw. All around people were busy, moving, bending, raising and lowering their arms, kneeling down, grabbing on together, and different things caused them to do it together. How was the common element visible, that which lay behind the purpose of their activity? He did not see it, and they themselves would also not have experienced it. What was visible of those who commanded them, the SS man, the men in brown uniforms, the know-it-alls and the demanders of all, the almighty voice and the flood of words were themselves only a sign, the origin was unclear to them—and one let it in inalterably, the deluge of words mixed too well with the deluge of feelings.

25

On the last day before his departure, after he had observed his mother packing his clothes in the suitcases, which seemed to him like coffins, Joseph ran off to the fir tree. Already from a distance he noticed that the small tree in front of it had been pulled out and was lying on the other side of the road. The hole was covered over with something white on which someone had stuck green pieces of moss. Joseph kept on running, he ran out to the fields, across the corn fields, and stopped only after he reached the air-raid station and caught sight of the soldier who had been observing him with his field glass. He had the certainty of being an enemy, an enemy among enemies of a different kind. He went back down the path of linden trees, shielded by the umbrella of green, fragrant leaves already covered with fall-like spots. He crept into the blind running along the forest. Pheasants fluttered up and stretched out across the fields. Beneath a feed stand he sat down and took out a small book. He wanted to give it to Maria Szmaragovska as a going-away present.

But saying goodbye to her took a different course. When he entered the kitchen of the farm building, the other Poles were also gathered there. Two military policemen were leaning on the bench near the oven. In front of them, standing upright, their hands pressed tightly against their thighs, stood the Poles. Maria Szmaragovska was pale and scared. The military police ran after Joseph, one caught up to him in the hallway and threatened to report to the Youth platoon leader that he was hanging around with the rabble. "That's right, that's right," called the chairman, who coughed his way up the stairs drunk. Joseph hid the Reclam volume of Descartes' *Discourse on Reason* at home in one of his hiding places in the attic. He found it years later by accident, chewed at the edges by mice and rats.

26

Joseph lay awake the last night before his departure. He would have liked most of all to flee from one bed to another. He heard his grandfather's heavy breathing, meanwhile his mother stole quietly into the kitchen, long after midnight he smelled the aroma of a fresh cake. Despite the war they still had the usual and customary things to eat, often more than they had had before the war. His mother fed two pigs in a pigsty behind the chicken coop. There were turkeys, and in the small stream next to the house the snow-white ducks bustled about. The mother promised to provide Joseph with these treasures. The food had long given the family a sense of self-trust, and the self-confidence encouraged them to avoid the proscribed one-pot dishes. "Other things are possible," his mother said.

Early in the morning the next day they sat silently at the breakfast table. There was a lot of laundry hanging in the kitchen. Joseph's grandfather held his teacup in his hand without drinking from it. Since the train to the city was leaving right after noon, they had an early lunch. Joseph's expectation was fulfilled. His mother put a roasted chicken on the table, the hunting room was set. His grandfather sat down, as so often, off to the side. "I like to be able to see all of you at once," he said. Soon thereafter the horse and wagon were standing in the yard. His father and mother carried down the two suitcases and loaded them on the wagon. With his brother and sister they got on the wagon, Joseph walked along behind the wagon to the exit from the farmyard. In the round bow window at the staircase his grandfather stood waving the large white handkerchief in his hand. He had already cried when they said goodbye and added: "I won't see you again."

Joseph didn't sense that there were strangers around him until he was sitting in the train next to the window covered with raindrops. The suitcases above him protected him.

After his arrival his aunt took the heavy suitcases from him. They wended their way through the crowd. Hundreds of soldiers were standing on the platform, commands blared out, school children were walking alongside him, the older ones seemed so menacing that Joseph almost lost consciousness. His aunt was able to find a seat on the overcrowded tram. She lifted the heavy suitcase onto her thighs. As she was lifting it, the suitcase sprung open, and the contents fell between the legs of the cramped passengers. The cake disappeared under a seat. No one helped Joseph gather up the things. The empty suitcase on the lap of his angry aunt loomed threateningly. Joseph smelled the musty odor of those standing around him. Their clothes were drenched with moisture. Joseph felt the damp coat collar on his neck. The button of his shirt popped off. The last thing he found was the toiletry kit. The nail scissors were sticking out.

By the time he got off the tram, the suitcase was stuffed closed again. After the door to the apartment slammed shut, he stood in the dark hallway as if shackled at the neck and ankles; he was confronted by the darkness and confinement before him. His body was stiff and immobile. The glow of the light came from behind, from where his aunt was leaning and giving him directions about where to put the contents of the suitcase.

That first night on the sofa was Joseph's first lonely night. He felt as if his chest had collapsed. Aunt Molly, at whose feet he slept, had forbidden him to cough. Curled up under the blanket, he thought about the entrance examination. After he passed it the next day without difficulty, his cheerfulness lasted for weeks. He enjoyed school. The way to school freed him from the apartment.

27

When the first frost came, his aunt put a Pullman cap on his head. Before he left the apartment, she pulled out a crop of the hair that had grown back and plastered it diagonally over his forehead. Sticking it back under the cap later on, or ripping the cap from his head, often brightened the dreary day.

Aunt Elly, the wife of his father's brother, went to the school to check up on him. The small, dark-haired, jovial aunt, whose heritage did not compel her first to conquer her own place under the new sun, concerned herself little with the hopes that caused others to impose rules upon children.

Before his first report card, which confirmed to him that he had finally been fully accepted, his aunt told him that the comment "Guidance requisite" would be entered in his student evaluation. He did not understand the meaning of the second word. "You have to be dealt with more stringently,"

Aunt Molly explained to him later. "Be glad that we have the Führer."

"Where there is no water, you can't go swimming; you all have the good fortune to have been given the water," the director of the school preached to the assembled students. They would know what had to be done.

28

Divine providence embraced them. The words were the water. They lacked their own life. When they raised their hands in unison in greeting or when they sang songs, which bored into them like commands, they were of *one* nature, the singing teacher said. He spoke to the living creatures of a common nature imbued with the past. Joseph despised the jubilation with which they hailed the unity and held fast to the immutable, to the relentless demand of how each of them was expected to act.

The errant and the false lay outside of that *nature* and offered itself up to be exterminated. The world should not be changed, it had to be purified.

His aunt, too, explained this day after day at table. With her turban on her head she sat there. Her good heart and her love had turned into fulfillment of duty, which guaranteed reputation and participation. One gained power with the power and walked more nimbly over the steps and down the street, as if after the Last Judgment. One had brought it about after a long period of being singled out, one no longer lay on dry land. One belonged to a party.

Aunt Molly had begun to notice that Joseph had been scratching his behind lately and that he had been fidgety while sitting. On the day the Russian counteroffensive commenced, as the krampusses were just about their noise-making and pranks, she accompanied him to the school doctor. When Joseph confirmed to him that little white worms were wiggling in his stool, the aunt's hour emerged from the body of the one entrusted to her: the worms, which were the most foreign thing to her, were to be combated and removed. While Joseph waited outside the door and his fellow students, who had overheard the aunt's conversation with the doctor, made fun of him, his aunt listened to instructions about how to combat the malady.

"No other student has worms," she said at home. His aunt became agitated because he did not seem shocked. First she cut his fingernails as short as possible. He was given his own bar of soap, his own bowl for washing, and an enema bottle. She forbade him to touch things, he was allowed to open the door handles only with his elbows. As much as he was shocked at first, he regimented himself all the more into carrying out the routine, because, despite being observed constantly, it gave him a wonderful sense of free reign. The halo of my worms, he thought, makes me untouchable.

In the evening he went to the toilet with a bowl of warm water, into which his aunt had poured a liquid. He took enemas, played with the water in his bowels, let it shoot out again or held it in. I have never been so much myself, he thought. When his aunt knocked and asked when he was coming out, he boldly gave her a time. From evening to evening he increased his dialogue with the worms, as he named his dealings with them. He had never before succeeded in fantasizing so freely—that would probably be a sick fantasy—about which the headmaster had warned him. In the meantime he gave the content of his enemas names, "the SS Enema," "the headmaster enema," "the Brown Shirts enema." The feeling of joy when he evacuated them made the world freer for him.

29

With his report card, his dirty laundry, the enema bottle, and some books, he left for the Christmas vacation. The snow was deep. A horse-drawn sled took him home from the train station. The alders rose up black from the covering of snow, which was marked back and forth with the tracks of animals;

the row of linden trees hung white, a giant growth coming out of the park. The return home and the repetition of long missed actions and encounters comprised the wonderful events of the first days. He felt himself released from the Movement. The Christmas holiday and New Year's Day passed by them. Maria Szmaragovska did not meet him. He also did not dare to ask about her. He saw a light in her kitchen, and also in the rooms of the Poles. When Joseph left the yard again at the end of the vacation, his grandfather was standing at the window and waved with his handkerchief, and Joseph sensed this time that they would see each other again. Upon his leaving, his grandfather had said: "I'd really like to see many more report cards like that." Shortly before boarding the train, Joseph confided to his mother that he did not want to stay with his aunt any longer.

30

At that time, because the snow was beginning to melt, Aunt Molly's husband came home on furlough. He succeeded in being sent to the front. "It's better not to be promoted," he confided to Joseph. Joseph observed his uncle's broad, arched back, as he shaved himself in front of the mirror hanging on the balcony window. The brown leather strap dangled beside him, and his aunt threatened him with it, whenever shaving cream splattered on the floor. This body, thought Joseph, must have been present when other bodies were killed, when body against body, transformed into insanity, killed as prescribed.

31

Whenever his lessons ended earlier than usual, Joseph liked going up to the Schlossberg. Looking out from the highest point, he saw the nearby undulations of his home town in good weather. He leaned on the marble plate with the compass arrows, knelt down, and looked out farther along the golden depression as the war had previously extended there.

They are no longer people inhabiting the border, they learned in school; the city had become a focal point, and the Führer would therefore reconstruct it correspondingly. The city was now in Mustergau. Looking over the city, Joseph imagined all the people he knew parading by him as models. The ones he loved were not part of them, and he thought to himself, I see people, and the pattern is insanity. If people would climb up even higher and see the earth as a ball, then the borders would fall, and one would have all of them at once in his sight, measurably and encompassingly in unity. Joseph had learned from his grandfather to respect borders. If one tears them down, what is one's own also loses its distinctiveness. How terrible it would be if there were only one type of flower. Live life at the frontier of death, they were actually much richer where they lived, because there had been different possibilities on the other side of the border. The border made love possible.

32

Joseph liked to amble through the maze of streets, above all through the small alleys and courtyards. On many a day he explored only one alley in search of differences. No cobblestone was the same as the next, the walls were saturated with countless cells of individual existence. Washed out colors gave life to the walls, cracks sent out branchlike paths in all directions. The worn thresholds at the entrances of buildings preserved the past in their indentations, which had come about through passing back and forth between borders. Joseph knew the residents of some of the streets, mostly old women who stared out onto the street from between the flowers in the windows, and who disappeared if anyone came too close. That would be torn down someday, they said. Light and air would move in, settlements of fellow comrades would stand here, brought about by the one will which leveled all borders. Once Joseph came home from such a walk and made the excuse to his aunt that his classes had lasted that long.

However, she had met one of his classmates an hour earlier, from whom she found out that Joseph was off somewhere else. His aunt struck him in the face with the back of her hand and, because he was bleeding, dragged him into the kitchen to the sink where he had to wash himself. Then he had to scurry along the stream of blood on his knees with the full wash bowl next to him and clean the floor of the traces of blood. Shortly before leaving, his uncle sat in the kitchen and watched as if in a daze as Joseph cleaned up the blood. Tears ran down his uncle's cheeks. Joseph sat down next to him, touched his uniform, and first noticed at this moment that his uncle bore that hated sign on his uniform that had stared down at him from the uniform of the gigantic figure at the dock by the pond.

"They've transferred me over to the SS," his uncle said. "I've had to follow orders my whole life long. Just as we have to cower here in the kitchen, so I have had to cower my whole life long beneath orders and fear."

33

On the evening after his uncle's departure, when Joseph was in the bathroom combating the worms, he hoped that he would never have to act as judge over anyone. Never to be in possession of a truth is better than to be possessed by the truth.

Aunt Molly did not permit Joseph to have a key to the house. Whenever she went out in the afternoon and he returned home early from his afternoon classes, he had to wait in front of the house gate. He sat down at the base of one of the cylindrical advertising columns opposite the main door to the house. There was still a bit of March sun in front of the house on the small square, into which several streets ran together. He immediately thought about whether or not his mother missed him as he sat there idle and useless, and then his mother was suddenly standing in front of him. And as if wanting to disrupt the encounter, his aunt suddenly showed up. From the argument that took place between the two women, he learned that his mother was going to take him to a home the next day. She had understood his wish, it was a moment of fulfillment, a time to celebrate. What had remained unspoken he, together with his mother, brought to pass.

As evening fell, his mother wanted to help his aunt and draw the shades in the rooms, also in the one that no one was allowed to enter. When his aunt noticed darkness reigning in her holy temple, she burst hysterically into tears. The precondition for wish fulfillment had been destroyed. Only after the final victory, when husband and son were back home again, did she intend to shield off the room from the outer world, and celebrate the family's contribution to the victory by candlelight. We were responsible if everything turned out differently.

Around eight o'clock he left the house with his mother. Shortly before his aunt had gone to the laundry room in heavy mountain boots, her turban, and a bright blue knitted dress in order to soak Joseph's bed linens. She was bewildered by the departure, "If you've at least gotten rid of the worms, then all was not in vain," she said. Joseph knew that his aunt loved him but had never learned to show love.

Joseph and his mother carried the suitcases and the backpack to the entrance of a swimming pool located in the nearby park. The octagonal building lay between fully matured chestnut trees. His aunt had convinced his mother to agree to let Joseph use the pool ticket that expired on this day. A shower before he went to the home, where he would be housed in a large dorm room, could not do him any harm. His mother did not dare object. Joseph went into the pool, his mother sat down on a bench with the luggage.

Once a week his aunt had sent him to the pool to cleanse his entire body. Mostly soldiers and old people bathed here. There was a room where one waited until called and assigned to a cabin. When the soldiers took off their uniforms in the changing room and stood there naked one after the other, Joseph experienced the stripping of a picture of deception, a distortion, a No turned into a Yes, into a recurrence, as if the naked bodies were stepping out of history and returning home. The more often Joseph visited the pool, the more undeniable it became for him. In the cabin he crouched down under the shower and let the water stream down and envelop him. The water that he took up with the enemas and gave back with pleasure and hatred, he mixed with a water that let him forget the affliction. There was nothing there then to frantically hold on to, not the future, not the past, not the present. Emptiness returned. The simple happiness of the boy who is only aware of himself and the world.

This time there was only one soldier present who was getting undressed at the same time as he. Joseph locked up his basket and went into his cabin. He left the pool. As the water enveloped him like a veil over his head, he observed it as it ran off. In a swirl the water disappeared into the hole whose edge was encrusted with yellow calcium. It was his first happy parting.

Hardly dried off, he left the cabin and sat down in the changing room under the fan. When he returned to his basket again and began to get dressed, he noticed that the soldier was peering over the locker door and staring at him.

Joseph stuffed his coat and jacket under his arm and slammed the locker door shut which revealed the body of the soldier, who was standing upright and dressed in front of him. His penis was sticking out of his zipper, dark red, full of hatred and anger. "I'll wait for you outside," he said to Joseph, took a step towards him, and turned around and disappeared.

Only after a group of soldiers entered the room did Joseph move from the spot. The soldiers' uniforms now had a more threatening effect, as if they were masked suits that concealed the people wearing them and glared out at anyone without a uniform.

Slowly Joseph walked to the exit. Where would the soldier be standing and blocking his way to his mother and lusting after him? Joseph ran off, and as he stood in front of his mother, he had the feeling that she did not love him any longer.

The shrill sound of the bell responded when his mother pressed the black button at the entrance of the boarding school, a moment later the door swung open, and behind it stood a man with one eye. His mother showed him a certificate, and he let them in through a second door. They walked down a hallway and then up a staircase to the second floor. They did not meet anyone. On the walls hung framed photographs of Party leaders.

Joseph pressed close to his mother as she stood in front of the director of the home. He was wearing an SS officer's uniform. "So this is he," he said and after he had agreed on the essentials with his mother, he sent them off abruptly and said with a commanding voice that they should wait outside. Limping from behind the desk, he stepped forward, walked up right next to Joseph and said: "I sacrificed a leg for the Führer. What will you sacrifice for him?" In front of Joseph his grandfather sank into oblivion, the big, blue, teary eyes were lost in the depths, his last glance indicating I am leaving and will remain this way with you. The creaking wooden leg echoed the screech of the herons. The director of the home paced back and forth in front of Joseph. "We want the same thing here," he said, "in school you learn, here you will be educated to be the same before the Führer. Everything else will be eradicated. There is only one wish, all those little wishes have to remain outside the door, yes, they will disappear. The heart's selfish feelings of happiness we must sacrifice to the seriousness of the whole. In the war we are celebrating our German sense of reason; if you ever become a full-blooded National Socialist, you will know that you are living what nature intends. It establishes our limits for us, ones we must obey. It must be the highest expression of our will to subject ourselves cheerfully to the order. In it all that is old will be done away with. You must give it up too. You will be assigned number 453."

Joseph had to go out and fetch his mother. He stood standing in front of the door. The long hallway had the effect of restoring the feeling that he could go. The black and white stone squares reflected the March sun below the windows. Because Joseph felt he was being watched, he hopped on one foot along the white stones. At the darker end of the hallway he was suddenly standing in front of a small man who had perhaps already been waiting there. Joseph turned around and ran back to the door from which his mother was just coming. "You can come to visit once a month," she said, "we have to go to the locker room, but after we go see the teacher." "I'm he," Joseph heard the little man behind him reply. He shook hands first with Joseph, then with his mother. "My name is Allemann. I'm the teacher of the division your son is entering. I'll show you the lockers, the sleeping quarters, and the study hall." The row of lockers had been built in a former chapel. Pictures of saints on the ceiling had been painted over poorly and were all cracked; the sleeping quarters were on the fourth floor, built into the attic. There were over twenty beds spread throughout the room, the floor was of stone. Two windows faced to the south. From them one could see the northwest side of the still barren Schlossberg so that the rocks, which were free of growth, shone forth powerfully. In the study hall there were twelve double benches and a desk for the teacher, behind which the Führer's picture was hanging. Otherwise the room was bare, only traces of dirt on the ceiling and walls stood out.

Initially the teacher declined the mother's wish that Joseph accompany her back to the tram. Only after Joseph involuntarily touched the teacher's arm and asked him with a trembling voice to allow him this goodbye, did the teacher say, "This is the first and the last exception." He received a leave pass that he had to show to the man with one eye.

On the way to the tram station both of them were silent. His mother walked faster than usual. Joseph thought about whether the time would come when he would be able to talk about all of this as a past event, but it seemed unlikely to him.

They arrived at the station at the same time as the tram. His mother climbed up onto the open rear platform and extended her hand down to Joseph once again. They remained silent as before, both cried unashamedly. The farther his mother's face moved away, the more open and more beautiful it became, and a place had seized him in advance with this departure in which happiness would remain inviolable.

The home was located in a side street next to the one his mother took to the train station. Beyond the home stood a textile factory with a tall smokestack. A wooden fence ran in front of the home. Behind it was an orchard with several small garden sheds. The garden bordered on the back side of a row of buildings. This in turn bordered a large square, the southern part of which had an island of brown stands selling wood in the middle. The houses behind them were not more than a story high, so that the square assumed the character of a village. This made it more homelike for Joseph, and he was glad that it was near the home. Before he went back to the home, Joseph bought a folder with writing paper in one of the small stationery shops on the square. The small, fat, blonde woman who owned the shop asked Joseph whether he was writing his father. "Yes," he answered, and his mother and his grandfather too." "So, they're all at the front?" she asked, "Then you'll soon be as lonely as I am."

Meanwhile the pupils had been arriving at the home. He entered the study hall. He went up to one of the students with whom he was in the same class, and a second one, also a fellow student, came along and greeted him. He did not know the others. At the same time several bigger boys came into the room and checked out the new arrival. Would he be able to give them something in exchange for their protection, they asked him. Joseph accompanied them to the locker room. He was sure that he had the New Zealander's chocolate in the bag that his mother had brought along from home and that he had not yet opened; he was also certain that his mother had packed bacon and smoked meat. Excitedly he tore open the straps. The bigger boys pressed in closely around him. Shocked he saw that a new Hitler Youth uniform with a belt and an airspeed indicator was lying on top, but right beneath it packed in wax paper were the meat and the bacon. As the older boys opened the package and one of them began to divide it up with his knife, he discovered the chocolate in the black corduroy pants of the uniform. The biggest one of the boys made off with it. The steps echoed in the wide room. He emptied out the bag and locked the locker. He had not taken notice of any of the faces of his protectors.

Immediately thereafter the bell rang, and they took him along to the dining hall. They told him that their group teacher, Allemann, was in charge of monitoring the dining hall. Well over a hundred pupils were present in the hall. Joseph arrived at a table at which he did not know anyone. He was happy to discover that talking in the dining hall was forbidden. They stood in front of the tables until no further word was spoken. "Everybody eat what he can, everyone," called out a captain, and the others shouted loudly, "Dig in." After the meal they rose at the teacher's command. The captain shouted "Allemann is good," "Satisfied," answered the chorus. "Once more," commanded the teacher. The scene was repeated once and then again. After the third try the director of the home was standing in the hall and shouted with all his might "Out into the yard." They had to line up in rows and columns. In the second row, third from the last, stood Joseph; jabs in the back warned him to obey the commands more quickly. "The novice will have learned before long, he will remain behind here to practice."

The hundred of them stirred up the sand in the yard, they coughed amidst the dusty sandstorm, and Joseph observed that they were all very happy, that they did more than the commands demanded, they exceeded themselves in carrying out the orders in unison. The small stones crunched, the dust fell on the lips that smiled as they exerted themselves. Each punishment was a means to improvement, improvement lowered the heartbeat, decreased the sensation of pain. The discipline was wish and fulfillment.

34

Joseph stayed behind alone. Another teacher, large, sinewy, with narrow lips and rimless glasses, had him run, lie down, stop, turn around, spin. There were many voices present in the sound of his voice, and soon it was a voice, a song, a competition with the truth, a "That's the way it should be" and a "That's the way it is." "This will remain part of you forever," said the teacher standing right in front of him, and, only after being boxed on the ears, did he understood that he was compelled to echo the sign of eternal acknowledgment and say "Jawohl." "Jawohl" was the preparedness for death, for preserving the one who would not die.

Hounded, he sat down at his desk. During the recess Instructor Allemann led him off to his room; he wanted to set up a file card and over the course of time enter the essentials about him. The teacher wore thick glasses. When he wrote, he dropped his head down deeply. His writing hand trembled more severely than the other. His limping gait stemmed from his left foot, which appeared to be a club foot. His hands were small, the fingers noticeably long and well-formed. His glasses prevented looking directly into his eyes. The room was crammed from floor to ceiling with books. In one corner large format books were piled up to the ceiling. "Those I read with my fingers; they're books written in Braille. I borrow them from Leipzig." He took one and held it in front of Joseph's face. "Take it," he said, "then you will know how important the hand is and all that one can do with it. The world comes to you through your fingers; books take you back on the road on which they have come."

On the yellow paper with the small raised dots, which kept the world inaccessible and closed off, Joseph's index and middle fingers bumped into Allemann's fingers. "We will get to know each other," Allemann said, "once a week when I am at the university, you will stand guard for an hour in my room." Joseph went back into the study hall. He did not say anything to his friend Johann. The encounter with Allemann had immediately turned into a secret. His fingers and the script were awaiting an answer, and he wanted to find it himself, silently, despite the loud voices. Before they went to the dormitory, they sat huddled close together polishing their shoes. Then they placed them in front of them on their desks and had them checked by the teacher's aide, a student from the upper class who always looked in gleefully and beaming because he knew that he would soon be one of the soldiers. He stood with his hands propped behind the desk, had sunk his head down, and had led the division through snow-covered Russia. Without wanting to ask questions, they followed the answer that was given to them and everyone in the room was obligated to it. Like the soldiers who had outgrown the bourgeoisie and Liberalism (at that time Joseph did not dare to ask for days what was meant by Liberalism), they also fought against Bolshevism; they were on their way to the true fraternity of the army, where their life would be united with the meaning of life to which they had subordinated themselves. No one should live split off, in remote venom-sacs, into the Volk the Führer would lead them to fellow comrades. "Youth of Germany," shouted the teacher's aide and looked up. When the Instructor Allemann entered the room at this moment, something strange merged with the enthusiasm, and the fellow students seemed like the texts in Braille. Joseph entered the dormitory sheepishly, got washed like the others, pulled down his bed in the same way, and crawled in, while others were snapping at each other with towels tied in knots.

Darkness ended the first day. Observed and spoken to from all angles, the echo of the day passed over Joseph, it divided itself, and both parts pulled him towards them. He wanted to hold on to what was sinking away, his mother descended into him and left him as if she might return only from the past and not from the future. Along with her he lost his place. The one who rescued him brought suffering, she robbed him, and he was thankful that she had accepted him. They withdrew from providence. He was alone as she was. But in disappearing she remained and was not defeated. She fled before the commanding glances. The other part drew him away to where they all wanted to go, rhythmically with clear eyes, happily, because by being used they could demonstrate their agreement in being the broad mass of people with good conscience for the man and for his men.

Half asleep, Joseph heard the whispering and breathing of his fellow students. Never before had he slept with so many people in one room. The sleep of the others was threatening. How long had he needed to differentiate the breathing, snorting, and whimpering at home. Breathing, that was his grandfather's painful gasping for air, his father's snoring, his resistance, his protest brought out of the depths, and his fear. The dead from the battlefield lay next to him as if they had stepped out of an illustrated book of world history, his favorite book, and had climbed into bed to warn him: you are not alone, there is no door through which we do not come and go, we all have a father and a mother, we do not belong to ourselves.

He thought about Maria Szmaragovska. She represented the foreignness that was near him. She read the books from his grandfather's library. He wanted to go to her with these books and experience another way of thinking, to uncover the way of thinking that had disappeared in Maria Szmaragovska's smiling face. Her dark hair blew toward him, and he pressed his excited penis between his hands and was shocked that he did so, just as in front of the stranger at the swimming pool, only the threat was more puzzling.

"Here's your Jew chocolate back," they suddenly shouted alongside his bed. "The writing in English gave you away. You expected to buy yourself protection with this poison." One of them pushed from below with the soles of both feet against his mattress. Joseph fell from the bed, and when he jumped up after being struck from all sides and ran away, he bumped his chest against the edge of an armchair that, along with one of the boys, blocked his way.

In the morning he reported the incident to the teacher in charge. He summoned the one Joseph had pointed out during breakfast. Joseph's trembling finger confronted wide open eyes. He knew suddenly that he had used his trial period, the useful desire to let himself be tamed, for treason. He had misunderstood the purification. The teacher, a disabled veteran with a wooden hand hidden underneath a black leather glove, struck the boy who had been summoned in the face with it. "This shall serve you in the same way as your striking of Joseph," the teacher said. "The incident will be entered in the file," the teacher whispered into Joseph's ear.

35

The next day Joseph went to school unaccompanied. He crossed the river, looked at the side of the Schlossberg, turned around to look at the people, he preferred to look at their backs rather than their faces. He had survived the first day in the home and was happy that school and home were separated. The way from the one place to the other was like a way out. Right in front of the school building the avengers from the previous evening suddenly dragged Joseph into a house door over which the swastika flag fluttered in the morning breeze, "There is no treason among us, we are not enemies," the biggest boy said. "You wouldn't betray the enemies, coward."

For days Joseph hurt from the blows, even though the ones who delivered the blows had long since accepted him again. They forced him to become one of them. They tore him away from his family and from the peacefulness of his space. They trampled his shyness with their shared conviction.

Joseph found the school more humane than the home. The teachers were concerned with correct answers, they rewarded and punished. During the course of the year new teachers arrived, women and pensioners. The teachers taught unobtrusively, because they were happy to take part in the war only in this way. Had they not employed the threat of grades, they would have been delivered up to the politically active students. Only the teachers who were disabled veterans triumphed and demanded attention. They denied the pain, they did not mourn their loss of wholeness. They thanked the designation, their sacrifice, that the Movement had accepted. In contrast to the groups at the home, the school class was not a real community. What connected them were the commonly wrought words used in the various subjects. Often the teachers used them only offhandedly, for the moment, with the noose around the neck. Several teachers read from famous speeches, they presented poems like masks. A can of food with English lettering that Joseph had received from a prisoner of war once caused confusion. In English class the English language was divided into a permissible and non-permissible language. The English of the enemies countermanded the English of the conquerors of England. The can of food was seized and Joseph was ordered not to bring any more propaganda material to school.

36

The students at the home, even the ten to fourteen-year-olds, belonged to the nation followers. For this reason, the younger ones had to fight against the older ones. To be superior to the other, was entry into what awaited them, it was the test of being powerful in battle. At first Joseph hoped that the uniform would hide him and let him blend in, but he was mistaken. Having been moved back, he marched in the next to the last row, because his white socks kept sliding down his calves. He did not have the look of resolve when standing in front of the flag.

Joseph and his friend Johann often asked themselves how the leaders were able to identify the suitable ones. All of a sudden they were identified, stood in the proper light, and confirmed the magnetism of the idea.

Envious of the call to be part of the nation of followers, which in the meantime the power of the home and of its director impaired, the latter sharpened his teaching methods. It had gotten back to him that several pupils had reported shamelessly the setbacks on the Eastern Front, that they simply exchanged reports and told of dashed valor like stories, like the battles of the Greeks against the Persians. As a result, they had to drill in all kinds of weather before breakfast, crawl on the ground, and do knee bends until they were exhausted. Once a week a sentence was carried out. Anyone who switched his worn reader with his friend's better maintained one had to have his pants pulled down by the others in his division. Bent over, he propped his arms on a bench in the yard, and the teacher cradled his head in his arm. With rods torn from the bushes in the yard, the students lined up in a row and one after the other struck him three times on the behind. As if he were purified by it, the one who had been thrashed quickly returned to the ones who had carried out the punishment, belonged as one of them again, and was thankful as before for belonging to them. The process of hardening was not limited to the morning hours; the boys were often surprised during class, free time, meals, and forced at night into the yard. Without resistance, without grumbling, as if the punishment were like food or other necessities, they rushed out and let themselves be steeled.

37

Shortly before the first extended vacation, Instructor Allemann accompanied his division to an athletic school set up in some barracks. The director of the home prohibited Allemann from conducting his own physical training and punishments. But he had ordered him to report every incident among the pupils. The teacher's sickliness and his infirmities were nevertheless a dangerous example, as well as the fact that he had studied theology. People had become wary, because the teacher occasionally contradicted, quoted philosophers, and hid behind the words of National Socialist teachings that were too nebulous for the practical among them.

In the anteroom of the barracks they took off their shoes; a tall, blond member of the Hitler Youth led them into the gymnasium in the middle of which an elevated boxing ring stood. He had them enter in rows of two and stand at attention. Without looking at Instructor Allemann, a stocky, black-haired man with powerfully drawn features came forward from the opposite side of the hall. His neck muscles were drawn taut down to the shoulder blades, his arms were waving freely, his hands cupped, "Here you will learn how to box and unlearn cowardice." He continued to ask who at this point had the intention of sticking with boxing, in the fall they would then have to make a final decision. Immediately a number of hands went up. One after another they all raised their hands. Beneath the compelling look Joseph did likewise.

Allemann stood quietly in the corner, his left arm, pressed close to his body, trembled, and his hand, as if moving convulsively, against his thigh.

On the way home the teacher said: "It's remarkable that all of you can be won over when one goes about it in the proper way."

Nature represented something different, it had the power to turn the one who was lost back to it, to expose the great words into whose confluence Joseph had entered with its flowers and growth, to drown out the one truth which had gone mad by means of sound and change. It was closer and was there in the past, did not fade away as the peoples' faces, was not mute, it did not press its strangeness upon people's eyes and place a seal on them. It was fireworks that freed terrified eyes. Joseph stood in the crowded train, pressed up against a window. He pressed his face to the window. Pictures developed in him and went over into the fields, into the yellow of the grain, the red poppy glistened, thousands of flowers stood on the meadow.

The lack of people in the landscape unleashed happiness. On the way home for vacation it helped to escape the words, the auditory images that blinded, the speeches, songs, and oaths. With the absence of people the wonder of the landscape showed its destructive superiority over the duration and burden of similarity. The ones he was traveling home to were those whose disappearance he feared. They were in no sentence which suggested the happiness of the majority. The family belonged more to nature than to the breaking forth into the Reich of a new humanity. Nature was wide, what was human was narrow. During this first school year Joseph's own voice was silenced. There was no excitement emanating from him, he convinced no one he was amazed that he was there, visible and touchable. There was no spark in him. He merely came to accept that the others broke out in shouts of joy and banded together, that they dealt with one another, as if only one force were moving them. The vibration of the train, the light of the sun standing in the west, its variegated appearance in the colors and shapes on the chain of hills shattered the confidence that he was returning back to his people, to his village. They seemed more earthy to him, those who had been forced to live there or had been captured, they taught him to have a home. Nowhere was Joseph closer to what was slipping away and decaying than where his paths lay. They ran through the familiar and the foreign, right down to the threshold over which he had gotten away from those who equated the world with themselves and the world as the Reich in which they maintained the order relentlessly, made it a duty.

Exhausted, Joseph got off the train. The gravel crunching beneath his shoes intensified his desire to greet his father, mother, brothers and sisters, and grandfather. They stood there and rejoiced. They embraced Joseph and brought him home in the horse carriage, and again and again they emphasized that a period of time had been endured.

39

The ecstasy of expectation, which had been passed from one to the other over a year ago, had gotten lost in the village. The ecstasy had turned into a lying in wait, which espied cracks and secret exits out of fate. The ecstasy bounded over individuals, away from those to whom the believers had once belonged as much as the free spirits. Joseph heard the voices of the individuals emanating from the inns. The emptiness of the silent listeners gathered around their voices.

Several of his classmates who had remained in the regular school were disappointed with Joseph, because he, as they said, had not developed into anything different. They even said that he was even more the person he had been a year ago when the headmaster had considered him unfit. It annoyed them that he had no tales to tell. They themselves had hardly had the opportunity to forge a path in the Hitler Youth. They worked in the fields and carried the milk to the collection stations. With each fallen soldier from the village they were required to work even harder. They were subjected to their mothers, they experienced fear of their fathers as fear for their fathers. For this reason they were thankful for the intervention of the priest. The gentle explanations and comparative interpretation spoke more to them than the teachings of the National Socialists with their shouting and demands, and who referred to themselves as "We Hitlers." They were afraid, not in awe, of them. One was in awe of the priests because they did not contradict the teachings, but they surpassed them more movingly, they spoke of the God the Führer talked about, incorporated him into the story. Even before a word from the Führer and his views had penetrated their ears, they hated the Jews because of Christ. The priests were victorious over the Party men, because faith predated the necessity of having to believe.

They shared their secrets with the priests. Among one another they knew no shame, they compared their penises and were proud whenever they convinced someone that they had already slept with a girl. They exhausted their imaginations in order to establish their lies. When someone offered to deliver the Spanish fly, they thought they would soon no longer have to lie. They stuck the squashed flies into the spread sandwiches of their fellow female students and sneaked up behind the girls, in order to observe the wonder of the effect.

The priests questioned them about violations of the sixth commandment. This was the priests' victory. They told of their lust and carried out their penance in full secrecy, before the voice of God and out of the sight of the Führer. The priests did not force them to forget and to defeat each other in combat games, athletic competitions, and military fantasies. They loved the sunrises, the aroma of the blossoms in the fruit gardens, the smell from the stables, they were proud to know the world within their fences, which made it possible to talk to their neighbors across the way. They did not cater to newcomers to their home. What was shared in common across the fences awakened their mistrust because it was difficult enough to protect what was their own. They were not convinced that the common weal made more sense than the fences. They wanted to improve their lot themselves, without the meddling of know-it-alls. In this way they loved their place, the immutable, which was already incomprehensible in the neighboring villages. They maintained their stubbornness and were proud of not being swept along with the times. A year earlier their fathers had gone along a ways with the times. All that had remained of it was that their fathers obeyed and defended the fatherland. To be a soldier was for them a question of honor and part of being a man. The duty to be so came not from outside, it was tradition. Their fathers were loyal to the nation. How could they have known that they would go off to war for a party, for the Führer of the Party? Their poverty had prevented them from acting any earlier or differently. They treasured the connection to faith, and it revealed too late the dependency, the advance toward death. Because preservation was the essence of their lives, they convinced themselves of who the enemy was. The soil of the homeland deceived them. Pigs, cattle, and breeds of chickens were the concepts, order, and boundaries of the world they lived in. Their watchfulness increased the economic success and fostered their understanding of the fact that the race is more important than the state, which prescribed duties and earlier on had tolerated too many opinions. The truth-sayers had an easy game with them.

Already a few days into the vacation Joseph noticed that cracks had surfaced. His friends told him who was an actual Party member, and it was always someone who repeated the same message. They showed him the silent ones who only worked. His friends knew who pursued whom and who provided favors for whom, who had learned to be evasive and to lie. The unity that they had created a year earlier had separated into clearly defined areas.

40

The chairman had gone to the race researcher Markhe and a few months later home into the Reich. The first Russian prisoners of war entered his empty apartment. Maria Szmaragovska cooked for them. The British had been moved to a different camp. They had refused to eat the same thing as the Russians. "I like to cook for those who are no longer needed," said Maria Szmaragovska, "with the meat from the forced slaughters I restore life to my people."

A few of the Russians hammered rings out of coins in their free time. Joseph's grandfather gave him an old silver coin, and Joseph asked one of the prisoners to make him a ring. He sat next to the prisoner, who bored a hole into the coin, filed it out, and forced an iron bar into the hole on which he beat the ring as he constantly turned the rod. On one side he made a heart. In the interplay of silver and ring the heart arched forward out of the ring. The prisoner stroked Joseph's hair and took, almost warily, the pork leg that Joseph had taken from the meat vat at home as a gift in kind.

Joseph took the ring to the fir tree. The path there had become soft following the thunderstorm. Water stood in the tire tracks. On the edge of the path horse-tail was growing. The green oak leaves robbed the light. Meanwhile, a beam of sunlight struck the water of the puddles and illuminated leaves and flowers in rapid succession. The fir tree was leaning slightly into the perfectly straight stand of oak trees. In front of the fir tree, grown up thickly, stood a bunch of impatiens, as if it wanted to protect the secret spot of the fir tree that was still closed off with its other name "touch-me-not." Joseph held out the ring to the still secluded hole which had been overgrown in green in the meantime, as if it were a witness to a superior memory. Here he would find himself again, and from the slipping away find his way back to the path which gives memory a future.

A few fruits of the impatiens were already ripe. Joseph took them between his fingers and squeezed them together. They freed themselves and spewed forth the seed, on Joseph's hands remained the traces of a bitter tasting juice. Joseph felt himself get away and simultaneously be bound to the place at which he found himself.

41

Some people did not like the fact that the prisoners of war seemed to feel more secure than those to whom it was still unclear whether they would gain more or lose more. Joseph had been given the assignment in school to ask the people in the village why they were proud to live in the German Reich. He soon abandoned questioning them because he received no answer and was loathe to ask those from whom he would have received an answer. It would have increased his anxiety about words, heightened his insecurity in using the words as the others blared out sentences and songs, as if the words would produce what was intended. He heard that in the adjoining regions on the other side of the former border having to speak correctly had become compulsory, like a testing stone, and that the Slovenians' mother tongue was banned. Joseph feared that these words of jubilation would enter into his language, he wanted to preserve its ragged edges, its unevenness, its clumsiness. For that reason he preferred to remain among the prisoners of war and the Poles. The foreign sound that they brought to the words, the confusions and mistakes and the missing words protected him from the language that overpowered. His grandfather was of the opinion that the great speeches did not really take place at all, that they only came into existence when loudspeakers were placed in front of the mouths of speakers. The words were snatched out of the air, and had only been forced into the mouth and pushed out right away again. On radio they had totally lost any human quality, or even any real quality, no longer would it be possible to differentiate what really happened and was happening from the events coming from the loudspeakers.

42

The events of the war had made many things disappear from reality. Joseph no longer heard anything about the Jews, who had still bought fish in the preceding years; they were gone, only their strange names remained as names of scorn. The Gypsies no longer played in the yards, the heavy-set women with children clambering around them no longer came to the door. Nobody had ever known their names. They had also vanished from speech. In like manner the fallen soldiers also disappeared. The names on the war memorials preserved those missing in stone. Death spun like a top, it did not arrive according to any predictable pattern. It gorged itself upon those who thought differently in the face of death by grenade and bomb, without war, without honor. Death lay lurking throughout the country. It was the guardian of the homeland, the proof of the truth. The death that was held up as honorable, that necessary death, allowed the destruction of those without honor as one among many actions. Extermination was something different than death. It purified the picture so that what was clear and ideal could shine forth.

43

Joseph started up a soccer team with his brother. They were not able to find more than seven players. He was happy that he was able to play with his friends according to rules without having to fulfill the rule. They tore apart what others drove to perfection. They failed in the face of the accepted standards. They practiced not having to win, and they were most happy when someone asserted: "What you are doing here is unnatural."

Towards the end of the vacation his other grandfather, his father's father, came for a visit. His mother's father was the heart of the family, his father's father was the head, the speaker, the one who lived from predictions, because he had a hard time fitting in. From his library came the histories of the world, which ordered history and delivered into educated heads a substitute for the lack of meaningful similarity. Either they delivered the world to its demise or to the interplay of demise and rising up or they followed the game of extermination through repetition and return or dreamed up the arrival of what was true.

Whenever he came to visit, his grandfather liked best of all to sit in the kitchen, eat egg dishes, and drink wine. His initial sentences were always some sort of prophecy. During the summer's most severe thunderstorm, as the rain lashed against the windows and the rooms became dark, he began speaking with the sentence, "As they now laugh, so will they cry." It was not enough that the Führer and his Party intended to reestablish the shattered unity with a new social order. Of course, the lowest in society, the workers, had been given a job, an occupation, and meaning. But unity was being imposed through a mandate, through war and conquests. The outsiders, the elements of tottering democracies that could not be reined in, that had not been in a position to create any productive stability, had only exploited the situation to quench the remaining sparks of ordering reason with dreams and impotence, force and infallibility, and images of the enemy. Thus the lost order could not be restored. The Reich was merely intoxicated and topsy-turvy, the most repugnant thing was the enthusiasm, the belief in only one human being. One could not believe humanity, but only *one* man and his army. One could conquer the whole world, yet a viable world would not emerge from it. In doing so, they thought they were obeying human nature and purifying it from entering down false paths, and they mixed nature with arrogant prophesying. And those who had used the Führer for personal financial gain, with the hope of multiplying this wealth, would have turned the lion into the lamb and inflated the lack of firm ground beneath their feet onto which they had been pushed after the First World War, with smoke. Old animosities were transformed into slogans, nothing really new was decisive, the will to descend into the circles of leadership was more evident than hope. The most tragic and simultaneously the most comical thing was that after the collapse—he did not believe in victory—that nothing would change because nothing at all could change under these circumstances. They would be losers and continue to dream of the order and of the power, or they would return coercively to the cause of the war and undo what had happened. They will forget and overlook what was new, in an endless trial, or they will no longer forget, conquer, seek something new, they will call on God once again. Even then, when the guilty and the accomplices are dead, they will keep their emotions in check where there was failure, because they cannot get beyond the cause.

Joseph's father shouted at his father, saying that the wine was twisting his tongue into a state of giddiness, that he was speaking as the others spoke, the way they all spoke. While his grandfather spoke, his mother prayed to the heavens that the thunderstorm would not relent; she even begged for the lightning to save them. When the storm subsided, the grandfather had fallen asleep, his head, enveloped by his arms, lay on the table. After the oration Joseph fled into the room where his other grandfather was. He sat bent over in front of the table; the wristlets protruded from his jacket sleeves, which he wore despite the heat. "How happy I am that it is easier for my flowers to bloom than for us to live life," he said to Joseph, "maybe that's why my heart is still beating."

44

As his mother carried the feed in buckets for the two pigs in the pigsty behind the chicken coop, Joseph felt ashamed that she had taken this work upon herself on the family's behalf. His stay at the home cost money, his brother and his sister needed to be cared for. His mother knew the value of hearty food. Bacon and smoked meat, sausages and bread, were summoned to help them persevere. The meat was preserved so it would last a long time. The smoke from the smoke houses altered the air in the village. The coopers had a busy time, even his father had smoke barrels made. If need be, one could bury them in a dry place. They were well prepared for an emergency, which loomed continually.

On the day before his return to the city Joseph helped his mother harvest potatoes. The field lay beyond the park. The yellow fruits glistened on the pumpkin fields. Russians helped with the work. The guard sat on a large pumpkin as he smoked. Standing up straight, one could see the top of the air-raid station. Again the field glass was pointed toward Joseph. In the afternoon Maria Szmaragovska arrived with a large basket of snacks. In the shadow of the horseradish leaves, his mother had hidden a small keg with cider, out of which the Russians were drinking. On this day without fate and history, they sat together and were people as before the separation and before the reconciliation, on this day without fate and history.

45

With heavy hearts Joseph's parents brought him to the train. Once again the passage of time lay in the eyes of his grandfather. What was lost was found as if the appearance had been permitted one last time. Early in the morning he boarded the train. Fog lay on the fields and meadows, the colored leaves were gray. Darkly the smoke from the locomotive mixed with the departure.

Joseph kept his eyes shut during the train trip. He pressed his head in a corner and pulled the curtain over it. He wanted to spend the hour until his arrival in darkness, as if it were something he owed his eyes.

In the evening the director of the home gave a talk to the cadets, who had assembled in the courtyard. The fatherland now needed to be defended. They would be trained during the coming year to be ready, they needed to have enthusiasm for it. The director's voice had become harsher. A year before he had talked about the glory of victory and not one word crossed his lips which gave the enemy the slightest chance of withstanding. He and the teachers would do everything to combat weakness, trips home were now allowed only during holidays. They would move against the outsiders. There could be only one will. The teachers next to him stared straight ahead. Allemann was the only one who had dropped his head, his hand struck his thigh. Because of his club foot his feet moved constantly.

Joseph was in Allemann's division again. The group's sleeping hall lay on the top floor and had been divided over the summer into two rooms, a door with a glass panel connected the rooms. Joseph had his bed in the first room, the wash room adjoined the second room. Here they would stay during the coming years, Allemann told them before they went to sleep. They were forbidden to speak after the lights were turned out, the imposed silence provided the desired entry into darkness.

Several days later Joseph noticed that some fellow students slipped into the beds of other students during the night. Soon they were all taking part. During the day nobody spoke about it; they behaved as usual among one another. Although some objected, even adamantly so, the sleeping hall was enveloped by a wall of secrecy. These walls of silence also extended to the other sleeping halls. They left each other alone in peace, did not go searching beyond the walls, and paid no attention when someone from another sleeping hall walked through. On the way to school, in school, during recess, or at play in the school yard when they formed other groups, it was a community of a different kind. They swore to one another, occasionally in blood, that each of them would report his first ejaculation and would then have to prove it in front of witnesses. This took place at different venues, in the lavatory, on walks, in caves, in clearings, or in woods.

School life had become more chaotic. A young female gymnastics teacher confused the pupils. The invasion of women into the empire, which the woman hastened, eased the inhibitions.

Many comrades experienced freedom solely as fear. They directed their anger against themselves. They became ready for sacrifice. But beneath the stream of denial for the benefit of the Volk and its Führer, the stream of longing surged in the opposite direction. The teachers were powerless against it, and also were powerless against the truth for which they had sworn the oath of office. The truth had surprised them and torn them out of their depression, from their normality, from the turbulence of survival. Robbed of the one great truth, they persevered and earned their bread as instruments. They were foreign bodies in a school flooded with propaganda, they stuffed the material into the pupils and used the unified world view as a threat.

46

The fellow students, who wrinkled their foreheads earnestly at roll calls and athletic contests, who heard the words as articles of faith and meshed themselves with them, crawled out of this skin in school.

In the home they enjoyed the physical abuse, sweated during the knee-bends, enjoyed it when they were stopped, to obey the "Up-up-march-march-pushup," they let the pain triumph in their bodies. What they would never have forgiven their fathers, they wrapped around themselves as chains. They assisted in paving the way for a higher man.

Joseph relished the hours when several friends found their way back from the tumult, when their bodies tore them from their bridled fantasy, when they withdrew in unison to compete with the lack that they did not recognize as a lack. But Joseph often used their unbroken convictions. They were able to support the weaker ones using their will as an example. On the evenings of the boxing contests they then seized upon the fights, so that those who were less willing to fight were removed from the battle before everyone's eyes. They were prepared and ready for replacement anywhere, where someone had to be at the top. One let them revel in it, fed their ambition, admired their protruding jaw muscles and the arches of their bodies' muscles. Joseph distributed bacon and bread to them and was happy when they helped out as teachers' aides. They were calculating and cold toward them, and they were simultaneously amazed that they were silent about the sexual activities in the home.

47

On Saturday and Sunday afternoons the students at the home were allowed to go out; they provided addresses as proof and brought a signature along that they had really been on a visit. Joseph got the signatures of both of his aunts. The one was happy that he had gotten rid of his worms, she even seemed to be proud of him; the other was rather worried because she had seen his teachers during their office hours. In the interim Joseph had turned into one of the worst students in his class.

Johann, to whom Joseph had given the ring the Russian made, often accompanied him on these afternoons. On their hikes they told each other made-up stories and escapades and spun them for weeks on end. They held back nothing in their tales that had neither beginning nor end. The stories built upon, repeated, or contradicted one another. They were happy that the story-telling came out as fiction. The facts that they saw with their own eyes shocked them all the more. The city was heavily sown with facts, but they seemed not to reveal themselves to everyone's eyes. The eyes took hold of the facts that they needed and thus often ceased to exist as facts.

On a late fall afternoon that was already quite cool, Joseph and his friend Johann happened upon a pair of lovers. He was an SS man, she a corpulent girl with a tight, bright red braid. They were just leaving one of the heavily overgrown paths leading up to the castle and slipped down one of the slopes covered with leaves and disappeared behind a protruding boulder. In larger groups they had fought their battles here against the imaginary Schlossberg bandits, had thrashed each other until they bled, destroyed tree houses, and also cut the cord from the flagpoles with the swastika flags and secretly brought them back to the home as lassos. Joseph and his friend followed the pair. His friend walked in front. He reached a slightly arched flat rock, lay down, and looked over the rock that was several meters high. Suddenly he turned around and whispered: "They're naked." Upon hearing that, Joseph excitedly took several steps forward and was pushed from the rock by his friend, who had just jumped up because the SS man had heard him. Joseph landed on his back, got up, and stood in front of the naked SS man, whose penis was stretching out toward him like that of the man at the swimming pool. Before the man could pounce on him, Joseph jumped down the slope and ran and ran. Only while he was running did it occur to him that he had seen his wallet lying there in front of him and that prior to that he had blacked out for a few seconds. He suddenly also saw the SS man's jacket hanging over a branch and the image of the SS man from the dock by the pond and also that of the deformed director of the home broken over the branch. Only when he reached the road that ran alongside the Schlossberg, did he run more slowly. Out of breath he stopped on the road. A man stopped in front of him and said, "Why are you bleeding like a pig?" A stream of blood the width of his hand was running down his upper thigh to his dust-covered shoes. Joseph fled into a telephone booth and tore several pages from the telephone book. He tried to wipe off the blood and cover the wound beneath his shorts.

At the home he cleaned the wound with water and put a bandage on. A few days later the wound became inflamed, the edges turned purple. In the classroom and in the study hall they were trying to figure out what was causing the foul smell. Like a thief Joseph evaded the sniffers. The lymph glands in his groin burned.

"You have brought along the foul smell," Instructor Allemann said to him. For a week Joseph had taken over service in Allemann's room, the watch, as Allemann called it. Joseph confessed to the teacher what had happened. He told Joseph that even a teacher had to be able to keep quiet and promised Joseph not to report the incident. He had Joseph take off his pants, removed the bandage, and took several little bottles and a fresh gauze bandage out of a case. For a long time he smelled the uncovered wound and then said, "You still smell like a boy, not like a soldier. Now no one will take you into their bed," he continued. "Maybe the Führer will like you as a result." He pointed to the picture of the Führer that was hanging in his room, as in all the other rooms.

48

The hardest thing to bear was Sunday morning. They were taught that these hours belonged to the Volk. "The Führer has not misled and deceived you," the teachers said, "we all wanted the war, we wanted this Reich, never before in our history has something been desired in this way. If you all now have to make your beds and undo them again twenty times, you will not be enslaved, we are teaching you what readiness is, we are laying out before you what is contained in our common wishes. We are learning obedience in order to be free."

The eyes of some were still gleaming, as they tossed everything from their footlockers onto the floor, straightened it up, and took it out again. Many thought they could celebrate the hero's death of their fathers in this way, undo the pain as if it had never happened. On one such morning during a break, the rotund, hunched, young Count Dietmar with the protruding canine teeth took the boys into the washroom and led them in their entry into manhood as it had been agreed. Simultaneously another fellow student, whose blond hair lay on his head in ringlets, played on his violin, and a photograph was passed around, one that Joseph had bought from a soldier at the nearby square and that was a blurry depiction of an act of fellatio. It was a picture made from a picture and perhaps from many others. The picture saddened Joseph, as he stared at it, alone and excited. It seemed to him like a photograph of something that had never happened, like the photograph of a dream.

49

One November evening everyone had to remain in the dining hall. The "Allemann-are-well-satisfied" was not shouted out. The director of the home arrived in full dress, with various medals on his uniform. With a mere glance he was immediately able to command attention. He was an ancient philologist. His oration started with antiquity. Comparisons led to the current cause, the German troops being pinned down at Stalingrad. They had to transfer the tense situation into themselves, each one individually, that they would do it in unison was something he would facilitate.

Several students had tears in their eyes. A shock changed their expression, masks formed in a split second, and looked like those in the illustrated readers that they attacked with the cold of ice. Had the director of the home divided them into two halves and given the command to destroy one another, they would have carried it out at that moment. The best of friends were already beating each other bloody at the weekly boxing contests. The battle for the preservation of their own enslavement was written on their faces, as well as the deep inferiority complex that they wanted to overcome through their obedience to the Führer, who was leading the Volk to glory.

An hour later Joseph's division, divided into two groups, went to the washroom with Allemann. They undressed, and Allemann, wearing a training outfit, stood on a chair and regulated the water faucet and the temperature. They huddled together under the shower heads, rubbed their skin against one another and provoked Instructor Allemann with their vulgar talk. The hour of celebration melted into the steam, the teacher was sweating; suddenly the director of the home tore open the door and shouted at the teacher: "Why are you letting them shower for more than the allotted time?"

Before shutting off the light, Allemann went from bed to bed and wished everyone a good night. He turned off the light and remained standing for a while, then he said: "Well, anyone who doesn't masturbate is not a German youth." They had considered Allemann a sexless being, a timid person whose acute near-sightedness limited his world, who was only able to read about the stimulating and secretive world of sex in Braille. Without agreeing to do so, no one from the dormitory said anything more about what Instructor Allemann had said.

50

It was not until Christmas that they went home for the first time since the summer vacation. Joseph was not happy, he was anxious about the return; the breaks that divided the school year seemed to him a time for things to move slowly. In school and at the home he waited in the background, but he was also about to jump off. On their wanderings through the old quarters of the city during which they also went into houses, he and Johann had discovered an old woman on the second floor of an inner-city house, whose window looked out over the glass-roofed court of the second floor. Despite the view into the open sky it was so dreary that the woman had a light on in her room. She had noticed the two of them from her bed and called them over to her window. "I've been sitting here for years, praying," she said. She took her prayer book and read aloud from it; dressed in a nightgown made of a whirl of lace designs, she sat upright in bed. She was wearing a large, broad-brimmed hat, which drooped down on one side to her shoulder. "Are you also Hitler Youth?" she interrupted her praying. They gave no answer. "Who is this Hitler anyway?" Joseph and his friend closed the window which opened outward. Whenever they had the opportunity, they visited the woman. Every time she sat in bed dressed the same way; when they saw her for the last time, she was hunched up there uncovered, staring widely with eyes fully open. They tried to greet her, called to her, threw flowers on the bed to her. Only when they heard pounding steps from the floor above on the stairs, did the woman move a little. The man was taking two steps at a time and stood in front of the two of them. Rimless glasses were glued to his pudgy, reddish face. His hair was cut short and shaved smooth on the sides of his round skull. Rolls of fat lay over one another. They rose up and subsided as he began to grumble. He chased the two of them away. "And if you are here again tomorrow, we'll cart you off right away," he shouted after them.

Over the Christmas holiday Joseph told his grandfather about the woman and her inscrutability. Like Maria Szmaragovska, she had turned away and pulled him away from the faces that bore the face of everyone. In her prayer she was absent and unreachable; she slipped into a crevice and escaped. Maria Szmaragovska also had the magic, she could differentiate herself from the others, but the difference could not be grasped; it was as if she were also torn away from herself. She was seducing him to go far behind that which the scales indicated as false and true. "The rats are most like one another," his grandfather answered, and with a sudden emergence of disquiet, as if a memory only at this moment had the right to be told, as if what was remembered was actually happening only now, he said: "Sit down, nephew, Aunt Molly's husband told me about a strange occurrence shortly before the Anschluss. He and several other policemen had to break into an apartment in the inner city, because it had been reported that an old woman, who was living alone there under strange circumstances, had not been seen for quite some time. After they had knocked in vain and had not heard anything but a strange rustling sound, the strongest one of them forced open the door with a shove. Scarcely had the door been open when suddenly with a paralyzing odor a V-formation of rats piled on top of one another, rushed towards them and between their legs, and because they were running away quickly, rushed down the steep and narrow staircase like a free-flowing stream. They would not have been able to estimate how many there had been. An intensifying whistle had accompanied the outbreak of the rats. Suddenly it became quiet, only for a few seconds, then they heard piercing screams from the street. The men had gone into the apartment, and only when they broke open the barred door did they see the completely gnawed skeleton of the old woman lying on the couch. They would later find out from neighbors that they had always suspected that the woman was living with rats. Eyewitnesses from the street had reported that rats had arranged themselves in a star over the main square, now named the Adolf Hitler Square, as if they wanted to overrun the city. "Now they are here, now they are there," an old man was said to have shouted, and since it had been understood immediately what the man meant, they dragged him off into a side street and beat him to death. "The police had overlooked it because they already been forced to overlook things," the nephew said.

51

Joseph's father, who went to the villages and also to the nearby market daily because the land that he administered was divided among the communities, brought home the news about those who had fallen. Joseph accompanied his father to families who had lost fathers or sons. He never heard a word uttered there against the war. Despair and sadness seemed to be only part of what had long since transpired; the war was the event, and the consequences came with it. Many continued to see God's unfathomable decree in it, others their sacrifice for the Volk. They accepted it humbly and silently or swore their "Now it is right."

In a strange way they lacked the time to react to what was happening. If talk turned to the increasing military defeats, someone was there right away who detected some actual sense behind it, as if the defeats were mere deceptions as to the ultimate goal. The less the situation became resolvable in comparison with the great expectations of earlier years, the more determinedly they went back to the mythos and to its way of explaining the relationships. They were almost possessed with demanding success from history, as if it were just moving solely for the Volk to which they belonged.

Joseph was afraid of the power of being swept along. It was impossible to let oneself be led by one's own wishes before the eyes of everyone, no one dared do it, to play with his own appearance. The illusion reversed itself and turned to stubbornness, they let what is true thus remain true as it was propagandized to everyone. They forced themselves to go along with it. In equal measure they sensed the urge to remain subservient, the Führer's utopia gnawed deeper and deeper into everyday life and could no longer be recognized as a utopia and defended against. Every action, and every thing, was consumed by it. Taken as a whole, everything was one in the end and maintained relations only with itself. Everything was a means to victory, life, death, extermination, clothing, trees and fruit, everything stood in line for slaughter and was mobilized for attack and for defense. Joseph saw how the people took leave from their treasured belongings and possessions, saw the shining and attentive eyes of the women who gave up their furs and fur-lined coats. "My ladies' clothing I am donating for the final victory." The children went through the villages with mite boxes. Sacks with colored metal were carried off to collection places, dried curative herbs as well. The exaggerated industriousness of it, the overdrawn jockeying to contribute, and the exemplary drive, the endless claims of belonging destroyed for many the ability to grasp and believe in values that were to serve the Volk. Some remained behind exhausted, but they adhered to the necessity of not asking questions. They did not want to be ungrateful for having had the opportunity to be able to become something, more secure, beyond the contradictions, which had made political involvement so uncertain before the

Anschluss. Now a person was what he was and if he was that, he was more than he himself was.

52

After a warm spell that compacted the snow, it turned bitter cold again. The surface of the snow froze, and it was possible to walk over it without breaking through. The sun beamed, an icy wind blew, and the snow sparkled so brightly that one occasionally had to close his eyes. On the last day of the year Joseph walked over the covering of snow that joined the meadows and fields. The stands of trees stood out dark gray, at several places crows were scraping for carcasses. Magpies swished from tree to tree. He came to a pond and met the Poles and the Russians there as they were hacking through the ice. His father was standing at the entrance to the hut at the pond. Inside Maria Szmaragovska was making soup and tea, into which his father was pouring large quantities of schnapps. His father was celebrating his birthday. For an hour the work stopped, and everyone was standing in a circle, eating soup or drinking tea. The Poles praised their country, the Russians cursed Stalin. Maria Szmaragovska gave Joseph a piece of bread spread with paté. She said to him: "Don't you see the absurdity that separates us? All of us here would like the world to be different than it is now. How pleasant the common slurping and the scraping of the spoons, the clouds of breath join together and freeze. Don't you sense how different the real world is from the real world?"

In the evening the guests who were invited every year came again to the birthday celebration. His father had the strength to celebrate his birthday. To have been born on the last day of the year, and shortly before midnight at that, was a good reason to point to the passage of time and to its return from the future of the next year. An accordion player and a trumpeter played in the kitchen well past midnight. Joseph and his brother and sister sat with them. In the next room the glasses clinked, and Joseph heard that they were talking about leaving and about the power of fortune, as if they could extinguish the sign which they all had followed. The dividing up of the pig's head after midnight was the smashing of a thinking head, of the one reason. One of the guests about whom they did not exactly know whether he belonged to the Movement or not (who knew what anyone could have been), got up ceremoniously and in his intoxicated state said, "I don't know what's better, to rot slowly or to be killed out there."

How close and hunched together they lived! The meaning of many of the words they used was entwined by the fear of actually not being allowed to use the words. Dealing with things and with oneself had lost certainty, the peace between words had disintegrated. The imposed usage separated the words from the actions. They obeyed a compulsion which spoke in them and invaded their decisions fatefully. Here they sat, right in the middle of a peaceful landscape, without the immediacy of the war. The wounds which tore open those who had fallen covered them with their memory. They took part and had not yet figured out what they were taking part in. Their eyes had not yet seen anything that had come to their ears; it was drowned out by that which constantly filled their ears. Their eyes became narrow. What they perceived was what they heard.

Well past midnight the guests left the house, each with his encrypted sentence for the new year. There were no clear sentences. Outside the bright snow glistened, the figures disappeared out across the yard. The crunching sound of the footsteps could be heard. The last ones to leave were the two musicians, the accordion player pressed the keys of his instrument as he walked. The notes resounded as if searching for a melody that no longer existed. The stars twinkled, they were puzzles in the sky. Silence mixed with speech, the speech moved like a giant platform through their skulls, on it what was visible danced, the same for all, the sand, the desert. Far out on the edges, though the world joined with the other, the truth became dubious, the will split, the strand tore, which wanted to have the sole right to rule over the earth, over space and its contents, from the great will, to rule the earth, and lapsed into extermination. The space which had been conquered for the Volk turned to blood instead of seed, fields became a place of judgment. The great will began to destroy its own possibilities which had become visibly cynical.

On the second day of the year the police appeared at Joseph's father's place. The headmaster had issued a warrant. The unrestrained New Year's Eve party had mocked the suffering and the willingness for sacrifice of the soldiers, "Our merriment is a game and an illusion," said the father. "We certainly don't want to stand stiffly on the last day of the year and suck in terror as a corpse." The official smiled, took a glass of wine, drank it, and said in leaving, "Well, strength through joy."

53

Once again it was the last day before his departure, it was again a day with his mother. Muffled, both walked diagonally through the park. The high snow covered the hollow in the fir tree. Their footsteps on the icy covering of snow could be heard in the distance, they startled pheasants that were flying up steeply between the oak branches to other parts of the park or were moving out to the fields. Joseph's mother told him that she had lined the collar of his coat that was rubbing on his neck with a softer material. She confided to Joseph that she now believed everything that her father had told her from the beginning. The war was devouring them indiscriminately, naked and alike they had been rendered; it was a wonder that a person was still allowed to have his own name. Despite the dire financial straits before the war, it had been a joy to live within the family; now they have torn down the borders, and smoothed out the maze of multiplicity so that all were alike,

like one piece of dough. She did not want to see her children disappear into the blank eyes of the community.

In front of the crucifix at the end of the path, where wildly grown branches set themselves off from the clear sky, they stopped at the spot where the earth did not turn. Joseph noticed that his mother was praying secretly. "That was for you and for those who have died." "Did you also pray for the dead Poles?" "Yes," his mother replied. On the kneeler in front of the cross the red swastika smeared on at the time of lawlessness was still visible, even though it had weathered. They proceeded from the cross into the village. They visited a girl who had gone to grammar school with Joseph. She lived in a small farm house; the front room served as an inn with a small bar. Set into one wall was the tobacco counter. The girl sat in the kitchen and as soon as they entered the room, shoved something across the table. "Why are you giving away the pictures?" Joseph asked. The girl then laid a box on the table and immediately thereafter a green and a red album. Joseph knew that she had the most pictures of anyone in the village who collected them from the boxes of Jusuf and Corso cigarettes. The one brand of cigarettes had pictures from the life of the Führer and the history of the Movement, the other the faces of German film stars. For both series of pictures there were attractive albums. The one with the pictures of the Führer's life had an excitingly written accompanying text. There was a whirl of collecting and exchanging around these two albums. Quickly an addiction for the pictures arose. The empty places in the album were seen as a mark of scandal. Joseph did not know anyone who owned all the pictures, but there were rumors that there were a couple of lucky people here and there who were not missing any of them. They seemed to possess the entire truth, the complete fullness of what was visible. Several pictures appeared in specific regions like major lucky strikes and were not to be found in the boxes of other regions. Joseph was still missing three pictures, the rarest one was picture 116.

Joseph had the suspicion that the girl in the tobacco shop secretly opened the boxes, took the pictures that she herself needed and stuck other ones back in. Joseph exchanged several pictures with the girl for his friends. As they continued on, the girl called, "Look here," and she showed him picture 116. On the way home Joseph's mother tried to console him. She was surprised that he was exactly like the others in this regard. "Your father is smoking more because of you, even your grandfather asks about the pictures in order to please you."

These pictures were the signs that they all wanted to have. The children's passion for collecting was joined to these pictures, as if nothing else but these pictures mattered, as if everything had been transformed into them.

54

At home they found out from the grandfather that Joseph's other grandfather had gone with his father to the church because the grandfather wanted to play the small organ. Immediately Joseph ran to the church, slipped secretly up to the choir loft, and observed father and son. His father was sitting on the bellows and pressed the round worn handle up and down, his grandfather played and sang, his legs, especially thin in the narrow striped pants, wandered back and forth across the pedals. The grandfather had been drinking. He continued playing one melody for some time, the words to it came immediately to Joseph's memory: "Quite right, what is mortal passes away, chance cannot last forever, in the face of its almighty scorn the worlds are torn asunder and are no more." When he saw Joseph, he interrupted his playing. "Listen now to Wotan's departure," he said. He began to sing so loud that his father jumped up angrily. The notes from the organ died out slowly, but the grandfather continued playing with hands and feet until he realized that he was all alone with his voice.

On the way home Joseph's father told him that the church organist had died in the war. As a grammar school student Joseph had often been allowed to work the bellows for him. He was the son of a farmer from the village and had studied theology. His grandfather, who collected organ and harmonium literature, had in his day given the young organist music scores and had played together with him a few times. Joseph remembered that his grandfather had once said to the young organist: "I have bought myself the most important pieces of music arranged for harmonium. With it I can fill up my loneliness with sound." "The world would have to be that way for one to transpose it for the harmonium," the young organist answered at the time.

In the evening his father took the picture of the Führer out of the room and hanged a picture of Vergely in its place. "My father pulled no punches when I brought him to the train station." The herons have torn the organist to pieces, Joseph thought before going to sleep, the Movement began to mirror itself in its dead.

55

Because Joseph had not gotten dressed quickly enough and took too long at breakfast, his father and mother went on ahead of him to the wagon with the luggage, which was waiting outside of the yard. There was only a narrow shoveled path through the yard. Joseph walked backwards as he left the yard, his grandfather was standing again in the bow window with the large handkerchief in his hand, his hat pulled down low over his face. He could not respond to Joseph's last wave because a fit of coughing forced him to press the white handkerchief to his mouth and cover his face.

On the day of full mobilization Joseph returned to the home. Already at the first roll call the director of the home, whose face had become more corpulent, shouted that the same thing was playing itself out in the whole and in every cell. He felt a loss because he could not send them off to the front right away. He took his revenge on the cadets as if they were refusing their military duty. He questioned them as to whether or not the teachers in the school had made reference to the need to summon all resources. He himself went along to boxing training and indicated who should fight against whom. He also stood nearby when the group leader drilled with them. At the home he had them do extra drills according to the roll call.

Now as before most of the cadets let all of this happen to them with enthusiasm, as if they had to follow the rumblings of a natural catastrophe. They remained encapsulated in what was happening. They loved the play of power. They saw themselves from without. They wanted to look like the pictures from which they were looked at.

Separated from obedience and the desire to let themselves be hardened physically and be tortured, they were driven now as before by the other side of their body to their shared sexuality. As if they would not sacrifice this one last secret, they contradicted the ideal of their whole enthusiasm. In this regard their shame before the face of the Führer was absent. They loved themselves in the others, perhaps even with revulsion, because even this love had the markings of what was one and the same. It completed itself in the secret openness among one another, even among the compulsion, with the fantasy that sprang to them in the dark, and they felt themselves free with it.

In a back street behind the square near the home was a small bordello. Across from it was a pastry shop. While they waited in line for sweets and devoured them, they watched the comings and goings of the soldiers. They made bets about the different lengths of time the soldiers would stay. They earned a little respect if they had the courage to go into the house and ring the doorbell of the bordello. They devoured the faces of the soldiers because they had seen the women's vaginas, and while they were nearby, only a wall was before them. Superficially created by the demands that they had to fulfill, raised to the state of exchangeable similarity, they wanted to free sex from secrecy, from the trappings of forbiddenness. They themselves had never learned to be more than they had to be, rectangular in body and soul, in order to be torn apart for the truth.

56

After a day at school on which Joseph had been labeled incorrigible by his English teacher, he returned with his friend Johann to the home. On the second floor where he had encountered Instructor Allemann for the first time, stood Aunt Elly, and he thought she had come because of the English teacher. She walked up to him and said: "Your grandfather died at home." "When?" Joseph did not ask anything else, and he did not wait for his aunt's response. "Are you cold?" his friend Johann asked, as he stood next to him. "The world is different than it seems," he said to Joseph.

In a matter of seconds, sentences, sentence fragments, grandfather sentences, father sentences, Maria Szmaragovska sentences came to mind. He himself was not able to utter a word. "We'll go to the director and ask him if you can go home." "Ask?" asked Joseph. The director denied the request. Only then did Joseph shed his first tears. "German youth don't cry." "You have to let him go," replied his aunt. She said it so decisively and without regard for the man who made himself stand out with his uniform that he said, "As an exception, what is one supposed to do with a weakling?"

At this moment it occurred to Joseph that the director had once ordered him in the mess hall to pick up a fork from under the table that had fallen from the hand of one of the teachers. As he was getting up, Joseph bumped the leg of the director with the fork. Startled, Joseph recoiled, but the director had not noticed anything. It was the wooden leg he had touched. Joseph then pressed the fork against the leg and reappeared trembling. The director thanked him and it was the first time that he smiled at him. "A piece of him is already dead," Joseph said to his friend Johann.

The next day Joseph traveled home on the midday train. The school had let him go without any further ado. Although having to die was more prevalent during these times than ever before and was divided into something both common and uncommon, and the response to death was sadness and pride, the everyday occurrence of death forced people to look away. Like the consequence of an order.

Conflicting thoughts raced through Joseph's head. He mourned his grandfather because he could no longer fulfill his wish of standing in front of him as a maturant, and because he had died without having known how the war ended. Then it was almost easy for him because the blue eyes were no longer there which had to mourn because of him. There was one less person who suffered on account of him. At each station Joseph moved to a different compartment. The train was almost empty. He hoped to be overcome suddenly in one compartment by the sadness, to be given a jolt, which would have provided him the certainty of saying that this is who this person was who had feelings. At the home and at school they had only learned to say yes to their duties, to say yes to the highest values that swished like rods above their heads.

No one picked Joseph up from the train station. For forty-five minutes he walked, proceeding ever more slowly, along the snow-covered road, and sank in up to his ankles. To the left of the road was the air-raid station, so well hidden that it was scarcely visible. When he was at the same height as it, the porthole of the glass cupola opened, and a soldier, a farmer from the village, waved to him and screamed in a loud voice: "My condolences!" He had set his binoculars on him as he did so. At home he found his mother in the kitchen. Two fully filled clotheslines ran diagonally through the kitchen, in one of the two rows his mother stood with a woman he did not know. Joseph ran to his mother. The embrace unleashed the expression of sorrow he craved. His back felt cold because of the unknown woman standing behind him. She only now comprehended that there was a dead person in the house. The way to the room where his dead grandfather lay led down the long hall. Down it his grandfather had gone into the kitchen. The floorboards creaked, the ice on the windows greeted like dead flowers, as if there were still an appearance that released the splendor of death. Between the flowers the glass house was visible, no smoke rose from the chimney.

His grandfather lay on the reddish mahogany bed, his rosary beads clutched between his folded hands. The suit was too large for him, the toes of the black socks were empty and sunken in a little. Joseph's mother led him to the glass of holy water in which there was a small twig of thuja. He had to bless his grandfather. Three drops of water settled in the deep eye sockets and glistened in the candlelight. The motionless body lay in the bed, the last look, stark, without movement, an image, a stone which entered into memory.

At the burial the family, the relatives, the neighbors and friends walked behind the casket. Two horses pulled the wagon with the body. The wreaths fastened to the funeral cart swayed, the flowers shriveled in the cold. The edges of the camellias in Joseph's hands and in those of his brother turned a dirty brown. It took over an hour before they reached the church next to the cemetery. After a short requiem veterans of the First World War carried the casket to the grave. A brass quartet played the song of the comrade. A speaker, bent over the grave, spoke in a feigned voice. Fulfillment, duty, inscrutable counsel, wisdom, homeland, enemy, and victory struck against each other like bones. His mother's face lay hidden beneath a veil.

Joseph wanted one for himself, in order to tear the mask from his face. The firmly frozen clumps of gravelly earth fell thunderously onto the casket. In the evening after the burial Joseph trudged around the glass house. Through the broken panes he saw the dark green camellia bushes growing up to the ceiling. The pale whitish trunks glistened lifelessly. At the edge of the stone water basin stood the watering can of his grandfather, who had disappeared from the world like a word that no one understands.

Joseph continued on to the vegetable garden. The saw stood still. From the barred windows of the farm building the Russian prisoners of war, who had gotten fat in the meantime, waved. In Maria Szmaragovska's kitchen a prison guard was sitting and playing cards with her. She ran to Joseph and said only: "You have lost much." Looking at the large steaming pots, Joseph replied: "Now the chaos is there in them." "No, no," she interrupted him, "the chaos is not in them, the head orders things, whether one wants it to or not, the chaos is outside. What could save us must now reveal itself." "I can't carry out any more duties, the head recognizes nothing." "It only doesn't recognize the duties which create the opportunities to be brave and terrifying." "All duties for which I have taken an oath make it possible for me to be nonhuman if I want," the prison guard interjected. "He also reads the books I have from you." Maria Szmaragovska accompanied Joseph outside. She glanced up at the Russians. "They don't know yet that they are beginning to win."

At home Joseph stayed for a short while in his grandfather's room. In the middle two black trestles that had supported the casket were still standing. His grandfather's hat was hanging on the clothes rack, his overcoat peered from the half-open closet. When he went back to the kitchen, the headmaster was standing there saying that he would have to earmark the empty room for the eventual quartering of troops. Everything needed to be taken out of the room that would make its quick occupancy difficult. A room must remain a room; mementos were only for the living. At this time nothing was more important than the present. Even the dead were there and fought, and there were actually no fallen comrades.

57

Just one week after Stalingrad had fallen, the cadets were informed officially about the defeat. They were forbidden to listen to the radio, and those who had hidden a crystal set were punished severely whenever one of the teachers found out about it. The filtered news was filtered once more by the director of the home. The teachers made no direct mention of the events of the war. They were paid to report only victories. When they were required, they repeated the speeches of truth without illusion, used the same vocabulary, and with every repetition their speeches took on the character of legal texts. The words conversed with one another, they united, because their applicability lay in their repetition. The teachers withdrew from their own voices. As if empowerment arose from it, they wrote what was essential on the blackboard and had the pupils copy it. Joseph told his friend Johann that Allemann had asked during the lesson check if he did not notice that the words crawled into columns during the writing and lost their rigidity, as if they already meant something else. They ran away from him like animals and left only tracks behind on the paper.

Was it the curse of Christian revelation, of the one incontrovertible truth that now the ones for whom it was a matter of spreading the truth from the beginning to the end gave themselves their revelation and left the world no other chance to be different? This once-for-all-time had come over the people and the comrades presented it its suffering, its joy, and its misery. No one trusted his senses any longer, no one believed that the sun rises, no one that the Reich sets.

58

Whenever Joseph observed the lips of the director of the home, he saw with terror how the words flew out, how the director began to speak words more imprecisely that he had used already thousands of times. Once in a while he also brought along written texts. He read out orders. He explained that tunnels were being dug in the Schlossberg tunnels and that the enemy rabble was being used for the common good of the inhabitants of the city, as if it were only a matter of victory over the mountain. They found out only later that enemy fliers had been launching attacks over cities for weeks. But soon thereafter they had to take part day after day in exercises to extinguish fires. They hauled sand and water, put the cellar of the home in order, carried down benches. The exercises were replicated in the school. Once Joseph even had to take part in a fire watch with a school group and spend the night in the school. He was under a leader who drove him through the house as if the flames were already lashing out from every corner. Now they even had to see to it that every lighted window was darkened. Light became the danger. What was dark and obscure established itself.

At the time that the words spread more incomprehensibly and the walls echoed with commands and proclamations, some felt that the words embodied an increasing fear there. But the loudest and most eager of them increased their state of readiness; their restlessness and their hunger for action signaled the approaching enemy. The enemy who became visible rushed into the prophecy. The sphere that inflicted wounds found itself wounded at its circumference, as it ate away at itself toward the center but left the spirit as a whole intact.

Those who were fearful now had to be careful with their language. The limits of language were the limits of the Reich and of the Volk. They had to be silent about what was passing over them. However, most of them believed that there really was nothing more to say.

59

In the spring they had been issued a green, squared-off bar of soap, which was called "RIP" soap. Already on the first evening they transformed RIP into "rest in peace." From that point on they no longer said, “Lend me your soap,” but rather, “Pass me the Jew fat.”

Once Joseph was at the site where the Jewish temple had been burned down. He had never found out precisely from anyone what was special about the Jews. He was also afraid to ask. But he knew that the Jews were guilty. As human beings they had slipped from consciousness. Even before the march into and dissolution of Austria, he himself had written the word “Jew” on Lessing’s forehead in the current script in the large format history book. Some visitor or other had told him as he paged through the book that Lessing was of Jewish descent. That was at the time that his father had returned from the old empire and related how Jews were dealt with there. Anyone who thought at all about the Jews knew that they were in camps or fled to the enemy in order to carry out their work of destruction from there. During an assembly of Hitler Youth in the city’s large music hall, the upper wall of which bore a continuous row of medallions with the profiles of great musicians, a face was scratched from one of the medallions and the name below removed. As if he were divulging a secret, Instructor Allemann explained to them that Felix Mendelssohn-Bartholdy had been there. “Merely because he was a Jew,” he said and they stared at him. After the performance the teacher took Joseph and his friend and two or three others along up to his room. He told them that his shortsightedness was of benefit to him. He could not stand looking at a picture for too long. He had learned to grasp an object from a few movements. His fingertips deciphered everything in his vicinity anyhow. He placed one of the large books on his lap. Joseph and a friend had to sit to his right and left and provide additional support on the sides. He read a poem by Heinrich Heine. “It is just quoted here,” he said, “because Heine is a Jew, and no one is allowed to read a poem by him.” The fingers flew gropingly over the pages, as if grasping into the void or as if snatching at a veil. “One senses beyond that which lies there beneath the fingers,” he said. "One of the Führer's speeches, read with the fingers, is not the same as hearing the speech, everyone should have a secret code." He looked into the eyes of the other cadets as he did so, and they laughed as if they had one.

60

One day after the call to total war, the evening boxing contests were terminated. The boxing instructor had been called up for duty. In his honor some final matches were held. Joseph reported sick and went to the infirmary at the home. In the room in front of the infirmary a young, dark-haired nurse resided. She had been assigned to the home just a few days earlier. Whenever anyone wanted to go to the toilet, he passed by the foot of her bed, which had a curtain around it. Right after Joseph was admitted, she gave him a few tablets of Brondosil. Only one other cadet was there in the room with him, a student from an upper class. He already knew when he was to be sent to the front. The nurse was especially concerned about him.

"Turn away when the nurse comes," the cadet requested him. Joseph knew more about him. His parents' house was not far from where Joseph was born.

The nurse stayed with the other cadet for a long time during the night. She sat halfway on the edge of the bed. Around midnight Joseph said loudly "I need to be excused." He jumped up and noticed that the nurse had her hand under the covers. He came back terrified and stammered, "There's blood coming from me, dark-red blood." "That's the Brondosil," the nurse replied and left.

The next morning Joseph's neighbor confided in him that he was in love with the nurse. He was not sick at all, and since almost all of them were obsessed with concealing their illnesses out of their sense of bravery, he had the most wonderful life here. "My father is an innkeeper," he said to Joseph, "I know from him what the people actually think, pure hooligans who want to have the hour their Führer promised them. Now they are talking somewhat differently with their hands over their mouths. Roast pork is becoming more important once again than the idea."

Joseph never even told Johann that a woman had infiltrated the home. Next to him the most secretive thing had appeared, even good fortune had appeared, for the first time the world had showed him this magic, something self-evident, something innocent. Duties were a matter of indifference to the cadet in love, he knew no reason to be afraid. Joseph often helped him out with bread and bacon. He needed both of them as gifts for the nurse.

61

At this time Joseph Goebbels came to the city. They paraded out in their Hitler Youth uniforms, and first took up their position in front of the Hotel Wiesler. "Goebbels, Goebbels, come out, otherwise we'll storm the Wiesler house," they shouted. After some time Goebbels came out and walked up and down the line. Joseph was standing in the second row. They shouted, "Heil, Heil," and Joseph suddenly experienced this "Heil" in him as if the other in him had been turned off. He was stuck in the pressing throng whose ranks opened up. There was no room there for the fearful, for anyone who heard such voices as a foreign voice, and was downtrodden, for anyone who stood to the side and filled up the emptiness with the people of his native town. He felt strange. In looking at this diminutive, club-footed man, at least part of the feared, distant speeches became flesh. On the next day as the open car with Goebbels proceeded down a wide street, Joseph burst forth with several others and jumped onto the rear bumper of the car. And at this moment he was one of those who was jubilant and whom he had so often seen in the weekly newsreels. A few days later he saw himself in the newsreel, as he was jumping onto the car. Following this event he went to the movies more frequently, three times in a row on one weekend to see *The Great Love* with Zarah

Leander. During the second show he was also able to cry. They were obsessed for days with Zarah Leander. One of his fellow pupils offered to be Zarah Leander in bed. They ridiculed Instructor Allemann. Their enthusiasm was repugnant to him, "Milk sheep you are," he said agitatedly, and they saw him smile with satisfaction, when the director of the home drove them across the softened ground of the yard behind the home, until they were exhausted and totally muddy, and spent the rest of the evening cleaning their things. Before going to sleep the strongest one in his division slipped over to his bed and said: "Joseph, soon now you will belong to us as well." He then took him along into his sleeping hall. There sitting opposite one another on the facing beds were the cadets from the dormitory. They had a condom, which they put on one after the other and then rolled up again. Joseph hunched over in front of both rows. He had to shine the flashlight on the one whose turn it was. "If you continue as you are doing," the strongest boy said, "then you can try it the next time too."

On the next day hundreds of Hitler Youth assembled on Adolf Hitler Square. Before the Anschluss rats had run over this square. Fellow students whom Joseph had told about it, were of the opinion that it foreshadowed the departure of the Jews. They had simultaneously taken along an Austria unfit for life.

They had been standing on the square for over an hour, and a speaker was shouting loudly as if he wanted to transform them according to the truth of his words. For the first time Joseph felt that a speech struck from the inside out, erected supports and pylons, and defended itself against the collapse. The sentences did not come down from above, did not hang from the pole of those in high places. The herons flew off fearfully. The adept dive to their prey was missing. A new enemy moved closer and was introduced to them, who was next to them, who was in their own ranks, who mocked the binding love and ignored the common wish.

In groups they left the square where they had assembled for home. Joseph and Johann ran to the old woman's house in order to see what had become of her in the interim. They found the windows of her room open; the room itself was empty and freshly whitewashed. A man was kneeling on the floor laying linoleum. They found out from him that they had rescued her some time ago and freed the community from an unnecessary consumer of food. They sat down on the wooden stairs and noticed that there was a door a half flight up on which the words "Society for the Protection of Animals" were written. It stood half open. Suddenly an old man in a shabby smock with trim appeared and shouted, "Come here, I have something for you." Then he disappeared behind the door. They followed him and entered into a dark antechamber. On the worn-out floor sat shrunken doves, two spotted cats were hiding in a single window niche, not far away a dog lay outstretched with a threateningly arched rib cage. "This is what the people bring us, the soft-hearted people," the old man croaked. "Take one of these animals along and nurse it back to health. The Führer loves animals too." Without a word Joseph and his friend ran away. On the small square in front of the home they ate a sausage. The stand belonged to a scrawny old woman who looked at them fearfully. "You can't say anything any more to young people nowadays," she mumbled to herself. "But they'll be whistling a different tune when the bombers start coming to us as well." With a trembling voice, uncertain that she might be turned in, because she was afraid of anyone in a uniform, she recounted that relatives of hers "out there" had already lost their lives.

On the way home along the river Johann said, "They preach to us all day long and we don't know anything." The evening sun painted the houses on their side of the bank red. The benches under the linden trees were empty. Tracks carrying rocks in carts that were then dumped into the water ran from the Schlossberg to the river. They heard the noise from the drilling, a new tunnel was being dug by foreign workers into the west side of the mountain.

Farther on ahead, where a small electrical plant stood between the road along the bank and a grist way before it emptied into the river, curiosity seekers were amassing along the railing from which they looked out into the dammed water.

First they thought something amusing was going on. But when they looked down, they saw a dead man lying half out of the water on a wooden platform. They soon found out that he was a Polish foreign worker, a little way farther up he had jumped from the bridge into the raging run of millstones. He had been seen running away from the tunnel. Everyone who opened his mouth uttered a hate-filled joke and attempted to outdo the others. A woman next to Joseph said, "They can work there in their homeland. Our men have to die out there, and they kill themselves."

Joseph and his friend were pressed up against the railing. From behind, the people just arriving pushed forward. Joseph sensed the pressure of the hatred and the pressure of the passion. Coldly, gruesomely, and inconsiderately nature crashed over the defenseless dead man as if its own indestructibility were assured by it. In their shared hatred the throng felt itself loved and protected. The dead man satisfied them. They would surely have dispersed earlier if they themselves had had the opportunity to kill.

62

"We have to kill the enemy, so that the killing stops and culture is preserved and then becomes final." This was the goal of the speeches that the director of the home gave; the relentless drilling and the banning of humor were also meant to serve this purpose. When Joseph took off his uniform before going to sleep and began the game with the soap again in the washroom, the strongest boy, who had given him permission to hold the light, touched his behind.

Up until the summer vacation began, time passed in the half-sleep of repetitious sameness. To the extent that the spread of the Movement began to pour in from the outside, the same "welding together of fate" solidified on the inside.

The threatening loss of all that flowed forth in terms of capacity for love and hate from the unconditionally desired ideal, and strengthened unity, and ushered in a mad sense of being loved and of open willingness to being used, reinforced the hatred of what was foreign. What was particular to a human being was not fathomable wherever it seemed to appear, where it sprouted up, one replaced it with the bodies that differentiated themselves with the characteristics from other bodies. These bodies crawled together beneath the covers in the home. In doing so they sank into distant safe havens that replaced love.

63

At the end of the school year the English teacher let Joseph run, as they say. She pushed him away, others as well, with a hateful glance, as if she did not want to dirty herself on machinery. She was actually an art historian. They had brought her in to teach because of her knowledge of English. She spent her time deciphering emblems in one of the city's great palaces. She, who was accustomed to symbols, hated the living, differentiated talent, the individual; she was indifferent to human beings. At the home and in the Hitler Youth they were at least materiel, blood put into action, alike as human beings with regard to their serviceability. They set pleasant traps for them, experiences were provided for, they were supposed to learn enthusiasm and amazement. For that reason many were dragged along, and able to be cracked open and set on achieving fame. On the last day of school, with their bad grades in hand, Joseph and Johann sat on the bank of the river beneath the weeping willows. Joseph's friend slipped on the ring. He wore the Hitler Youth insignia on the lapel of his red checkered coat. "I'd like to see the same thing sometime," said Joseph. "What is shared in common we never see, what we hear about most of the time, and we all obey it." "When I am at my parents'," his friend responded, "I think I am waking up from a dream. I rise from the water, in which we are swimming here, and dry myself off. My parents are then parents and this other world has disappeared, even their Party insignia is only theirs." "Do you also believe that your parents are immortal?" asked Johann. "My mother," Joseph answered. "Since we tagged along behind Goebbels, I've been ashamed to face my mother, Joseph, we cried on account of an actress." "I am also ashamed that this older student came to my bed. They want to tear us away," Joseph answered.

64

The bright days of summer over the blossoming meadows, over the fields of yellow rape, over the brown grain, the poppy, over the thick corn fields, were days on which the world stood still. The growing threat, the irritated indifference of the people, the hectic mending of the gaps in the truth with augmented truth, with controlled speech, with more invasive pictures, preserved nevertheless the same conditions. Death and atrocity were released like tame animals living among them. They presented material for stories. Where the war had not yet unleashed its destruction, time spread itself out, boredom suppressed any sense of emergency, the Movement yawned. The functionaries of the NSDAP looked for reasons to meddle, the sympathy visits, the overseeing of assemblies did not fulfill them. The puzzle of who was still like them and thought and who already disappeared behind the mask was one they were not capable of solving, they had gone too far across the border of the other. With the decrease in enthusiasm, their own truth became dark, but that made it even more dangerous. The farmers forgot themselves in the battle over grain and milk, and those fallen in battle were useful in diverting suspicion away from families. The Church participated in this double game. The rise of the Movement leveled off back into the condition which had lured them to rise up. The idea was turned into a stonelike formula of hope before it had been able to escape alive.

"They will remain as they were," said Maria Szmaragovska, "this is a long history, and history has time." Joseph tried to tell Maria Szmaragovska about the home and the school. She refused to listen to it. "Forget it now, you will have to deal with it your whole life long in other ways. That's when you will need the strength to fight against it."

65

In midsummer the soldiers and the leaders of the NSDAP were jolted out of their boredom. The enemy appeared in the sky, day after day the signs cut wounds in it. Dull sounds of motors began to roar. "Now we are totally part of the whole again and are no longer disadvantaged and without the opportunity to do deeds and to let the will reemerge," said the mayors, the local leaders, and the leaders of the local farmers. There was one single person in the village who offered resistance in his own way. When he arrived on furlough, he talked about the camps and about those persecuted. People suspected that he was sympathetic toward the enemy and aided the opposition. Sometimes he visited Joseph's father and stayed half the night. At first his parents thought he was exaggerating, later on they came to believe him. Although some people tried to take legal action against him, they were unsuccessful. He irritated them with his smile and went back to the front again. The residents of the village were glad that they felt afraid in his presence. When he asked at the inn what they had to say about the fact that the Duce had been overthrown, no one answered him. They simply accepted it as one does a thunderstorm, a cloudburst, or illnesses, and began to believe in miracles, and the loyal ones said, it could not all have been in vain. Worries began to divide families from one another. The fear multiplied the lie. The lie gave rise to the appearance that now as before everyone stood behind the Movement. The lie, the public confession caused by fear, was occasionally a form of resistance for the people living around the village as well. For reasons of religious conviction, many people helped prisoners of war and deportees. "How is meaningful opposition supposed to develop?" his father's father had asked in one of his kitchen talks. "Who of you has any idea what this National Socialism in which you believe really is? Only people's emotions have been mobilized but not their heads. Without knowing anything about the opposite, without becoming familiar with it, a person has no understanding at all of his own convictions. Since the First World War there have been storms only of emotion, but no clear thought, just as little in the cities as out in the countryside, and the ones who were able to think or might be able to think they have silenced like boisterous children or insane people. Where the highest value is health, there is no room for thinking."

66

During the drive home from a summer festival for the farm workers and employees, a tractor crashed. The wagon carrying some of those attending came to rest in a curve against the wall of a barn. A Polish worker, slightly drunk like the others, was driving the tractor. When Joseph's father and mother got to the scene of the accident by motorcycle, two rural policemen, the group leader, and the headmaster on a motorcycle with sidecar were already there. The latter acted as self-proclaimed guardian of the law at the site. Immediately several people had gathered at the inn across from where the accident had taken place and paid no attention to the accident and the injured, but only to the Pole who was held responsible. Joseph's father was in a quandary. He had opposed the ordinance that the Poles be prohibited from drinking alcohol or frequenting the inns. The policemen arrested the Pole before the injured were attended to. Maria Szmaragovska was kneeling beside one of the injured Polish women. Wracked with pain, the woman cursed those milling around and pleaded for a priest. The gawking farm women were surprised, for they had thought that the Poles were godless. They could not send for the priest because the Poles were forbidden from having any contact with the church. The priests adhered to this ordinance and saw no contradiction in it. The distinction between German and Polish souls did not disturb anyone's prayers. The injured Polish woman was cared for and was back in the fields again after several weeks. The arrested driver of the tractor was sent to a work camp. His possessions were burned in the yard at the farm building. The local authorities who had stood up for the driver of the tractor prevented the case from reaching wider circles.

67
Joseph visited the fir tree at the end of the vacation. Someone had cleared the brush from around it because placards were hanging on the fir tree for the schoolchildren and churchgoers who passed by. The hole had disappeared behind exhortations and warnings. Joseph had spent the summer outdoors with his brother and friends. They had gone hunting with his father. At home they were untouched by the lofty language of wishes and commands, by engines and the loud noise, which drowned out Joseph's own voice and that of his father, mother, family, village, and locality. At home the "I" fit into the resistance, into embraces, into the "blows." The ego waited, it experienced itself surrounded by its skin, it engaged in the game. Pure accessibility and controlled powerlessness waited before the door during the vacations. They lived, they were not dead, they were happy at being able to take a breath uninhibitedly. The food packages his mother so carefully put together for the city always conveyed with them the feeling of being something essential that was untouchable. The unmistakable smell of home heightened the hope of being over the threshold and possessing the unachievable. In the proximity

of his parents, Joseph relished being sickly, eccentric, contrary. Once, at night, when he got up and turned on the light next to his bed, he saw the face of the Führer on the wrapper of a newspaper as that of a man among men, without the compulsion of seeing only the Führer. The face blended in with the typical faces and was lost in the lack of differentiation.

The next morning his parents' faces and those of his brother and sister seemed more vivid to him, as if they had been temporarily rescued and protected. They melded together into one picture; they came together as nature, rose up like the compulsionless appearance on walks and did not look away, did not wince or pursue a point of view.

Joseph kept his textbooks and notebooks in his grandfather's empty room. He would have liked to live there, but did not do so because he encountered his grandfather in the emptiness.

The time arrived to pack his bags again and leave. With his notebooks and textbooks, he took a piece of the emptiness along, as a piece of free space for later on, as something invisible, a void, that belonged only to him and in which having to take part in the uniformity dissipated. Colored wash was hanging in the grandfather's bay window as he drove off. Again they accompanied him to the train station, this time more fearfully, because air attacks were anticipated. Upon farewell they did not say "Learn well" but rather "Protect yourself, run quickly to the cellar, get beneath the arches."

At the town railroad station he noticed that new signs had been added to the many already there. The threatening, open sky against which there was no protection, which evaded the power, required the subterranean as protection and hiding place. It was already dark when Joseph arrived. Through narrow slits a little light entered. The lamps, the providers of light, had been given the task of simultaneously diminishing the light. Military police passed back and forth in the train station hall. People were stopped and papers demanded.

Joseph was one of the last ones to return from the holidays. He had to report immediately to the dining hall. The director of the home read aloud the new house rules. They sounded as if from now on they were defending a fortress. The strictest rules applied to the way to school. Although talking was forbidden in the dormitory after lights were out, the boys talked until late into the night. In the dormitory there was almost total darkness. Measures to ensure darkness had been applied during the vacation and let no light through. The starry heavens were enemy territory. There was talk of death and destruction. Several of the older boys who had left the home at the end of the school year with their diplomas had already been killed. Long after midnight the alarm blared. A new, burly instructor, who was equal in rank to Instructor Allemann, tore open the door and shouted: "Get dressed, down to the cellar, air conservation exercise, take your blankets along!"

It took a long time until everyone had understood that the teachers made no distinction between exercises and the real thing. The director of the home, in full uniform, ranted and raved in the cellar and spoke about the cancerous ulcer of being soft. Over an hour passed before they were allowed back to their beds.

Not fully rested, they sat in school. Announcements and commands, warnings and threats lumped themselves into the fact to which their attention was drawn: the demise of individual will was now final. At the most they were only parts, the field of forces would reach out and grab them. It seemed as if they were nothing but disruptive forces, everywhere they were lying in wait for mistakes and saw in each mistake a threat to their insanity. To the same degree they ruled also over themselves; out of fear they permitted themselves no deviation and were resolved to nip in the bud the observable deviations outside themselves. They wanted things to stay the way they were because they had practiced renunciation. Forcefully they avoided believing that the foundation of their order was trembling. They fought off the thought that they might be happier in other circumstances. They denied it to themselves and above all denied it in front of others. Cowardice turned to inflexibility and strength of character, blindness to ecstasy in the face of the radiating idea. But the means of combating the enemy that were unleashed, the hatred and the possibility of also killing the enemy, undermined the community, which broke out in tears as once in its feelings of affection for the Führer or his picture. The killing, the clear presence of scapegoats, the beatings, the RIP soap passing from hand to hand, destroyed life together, the great power commanded itself. Those subject directly to the commands, soldiers, students, foreign workers, remained those areas that continued to have to tolerate the appearance of total order as such. The killing and the destruction, unleashed as never before and interwoven in the culture as never before, one entrusted to the strongest, indeed transferred it to the secret weapon about which they were now talking, and which moved up alongside the Führer as a helper, and seemed more reliable than any individual. And in the little things many still made their contribution to the visible outbreak of the destructive forces. Teachers and educators hoped that they were storing up energy for the decisive hour with their contribution to the radical order. But no one was capable any longer of distinguishing the walls from the facades.

68

It seemed to Joseph that the only remnant of affection lay in the proximity of Instructor Allemann. The students' affection consisted of the fact that they tormented the teacher. They took their revenge on him for their sacrifices. His voice was so soft that his directives were never followed. With their affection they delivered him up to danger. They laid him bare, they drew the attention of the director of the home to the fact that a teacher could also be different. He was the only one who was different. Their trust in him consisted in the fact that they made him insecure whenever they could. They talked to him as to a father confessor whom one uses to at least verbalize one's sins. He was genderless like a priest. They expected no reaction from him. Joseph knew that on Sundays Allemann went with one or the other student to visit his parents. In this way they were supposed to experience the human side of the home.

The strongest of the boys no longer forced Joseph to come to the other sleeping hall in order to be present at the common games. Joseph had gotten hold of some condoms and put them into his wallet. With the greatest excitement he gave one of them to the nurse's friend. Now whenever he saw the nurse, he felt a part of her, he had touched something that had touched her. In the sleeping hall the students were often lying in one bed, mostly after the spontaneous air-raid drills. Silently they gave each other warmth. Despite the darkness they pressed their eyes shut during it, as if they would be able to forget who was lying next to them in this way. Alternately they felt like man or woman, they would have all most preferred to be women. The most perverse endurance exercises, the most ambitious athletic competitions, the military drills pushed to the extreme, and the reports about heroes and terror did not diminish their desire, as it were, equally separated from their life to give themselves this second life. A song rose up in them that they did not understand, that they suppressed day after day with obscenities, as they continued, ever more crudely, to live their waking life, their life outside of the darkness. They armed themselves with sticks and kept them hidden in their knickerbockers. With razors they cut up garden hoses which watered the grounds at the castle, where the security of the tunnels triumphed over the skies. They stuck fresh reeds into the hoses. On Sundays they ambushed other boys or went up as a group to the Schlossberg. They became tougher, when they marched off to the assemblies of comrades. They scared old women, told them about the horrors of bombing attacks, and drove them to panic by telling them of recently heard reports that air attacks were expected. They rejoiced over the increasing number of air-raid alarms. They destroyed the order. If there was advance warning, they stormed home from school or sought out the Schlossberg tunnels and carried on their mischief there fearlessly. The air raid alarm and the bombers in the sky, the exploding flak grenades, and the long searching fingers of the searchlights became the higher power. Against them the teachers, the instructors, the director of the home, the high functionaries were powerless.

The air raid alarm bestowed a strange sense of freedom. Like thunderstorms, clouds, rain, and snow the bombers came; the brumming and roaring of the motors caused the windows to rattle. Now most people had the feeling of really belonging again to the entire Volk. It renewed the readiness to fight, heightened the desire to give themselves over entirely to holding out.

Joseph thought he knew when they were only playing along and when they were detached from it. But who did not think like that?

69

One night Joseph was hungry. He sneaked through the adjacent sleeping hall into the cloak room and fetched himself a piece of bread and half of a smoked sausage, the supplementary sustenance provided by his parents. It was strictly forbidden to wander about the building at night. He walked past Allemann's door. There was still a light burning behind it. Softly, Allemann's voice hummed. As he entered the adjoining sleeping hall on the way back, he saw that the boys had turned on the flashlight again and were playing the protective game of passion, as they now called the game with the condoms. Hunched over, Joseph whisked by without taking a good look inside. Just as he crawled into his bed again, the door to the sleeping hall opened. Instructor Siegmund, whom they had heard was a boxer and was now studying medicine, entered quietly. He paused for a moment, then he seemed to tiptoe to the door with the glass window. The closer he came, the more distinctly Joseph saw him, the flashlight gave off enough light. Joseph thought about calling out as if waking from a dream to warn the others. But he remained lying there as if paralyzed and could hardly breathe. The instructor remained standing at the door for several minutes, peered through the glass with his head bent slightly forward, then tore open the door, turned on the light and lashed out at the perpetrators, as they were later called, with skilled and practiced force. Joseph heard the bodies fall; however, he heard no screaming and no talking back. Over the noise and falling bodies, the voice of Instructor Siegmund roared, "You swine, just wait." Meanwhile everyone in the dormitory had woken up, and after the instructor was back outside and no bed had two friends in it, not a sense of defeat, but of triumph, arose.

On the next day it seemed as if nothing were going to happen. But in the afternoon they heard that the director was going with the instructors—Allemann was not along with them—from study room to study room. Towards evening they came into Joseph's room. The boys jumped up more quickly than usual and were ready for an order. The director's voice was already hoarse. He said, "You are now almost the youngest group to whom I am speaking. Someone is responsible for instigating and leading what has transpired in this dormitory and for whatever else like it happens. That person is someone who is corrupting you and rendering you useless." During the course of the day several students seemed to have betrayed the nightly happenings, the remnants of their secret desires.

The director spoke so openly that it had a great impact on them. They were moments without threats, the appeal to higher authorities was missing, he talked about the matter at hand, how they felt it as an urge within them, it was a matter for them to deal with, it was not a matter of duty. The director, it seemed, was not judging the affair morally: Volk, blood, and God remained off to the side. "True pleasure exists only with a woman," was the closing remark, and he would have gone out with the instructors, if the young count in the last row had not begun to laugh hysterically. The director yanked him out of the formation and addressed him imperiously. The young count continued to laugh even more perversely and mussed up his hair; his protruding teeth stuck out between his lips like weapons. Instructor Siegmund struck him in the face twice. Then the director shouted: "These are the consequences, you are more depraved and your health more endangered than I thought. Your spirit is also damaged and your sense of duty. This impudence borders on treason."

Only the second night after that did they finally find out what the director and the instructors were planning. At two in the morning both the director and the instructors burst open the doors, turned on the lights, and commanded them from their beds. They had to take off their pajamas and show their socks as well as the white handkerchiefs; the covers were to be pulled down and the sheets visible. "Semen control," shouted Instructor Siegmund.

The next day the tainted ones had to report individually to the director. The nightly raids recurred at irregular intervals. But the cadets did not respond with fear and admissions of guilt. Somehow or other what was victorious was their game, their individual lives, the remaining remnants of what was their own, their share of instinct still perceivable to them, of another whole, of a nature that in their experience did not subjugate but liberate.

They had received an audible voice and returned to their fellowman something audible in place of something inhuman. They had elevated themselves above the sacrifices.

Instructor Allemann was not privy to these events. The director and the other teachers did not consider his manliness and ability to see things through as adequate to master the so-called aberrations. He paced back and forth smiling in front of beds as the boys prepared for bed. Once he said, to the surprise of all, "One would have to install motion detectors in your beds." This was the second inexplicable fissure in his picture. As Joseph attended to his chores in Allemann's room, Allemann once came back early and queried Joseph with obvious curiosity. Almost as if coercively detained, Joseph sketched out for him the scene that led to the discovery and also told him that this event had nothing to do with the other encounters that had also taken place outside of the home in the interim. Joseph had to promise him that in the future he would continue to tell him exactly what transpired. Joseph found out that other boys, too, were questioned by Allemann in the same fashion, and that he also asked them to keep him informed of the most recent developments.

70

During the Christmas holidays Joseph slept more soundly than ever before in his life. Finally there was only his brother Hans next to him. The breathing of his parents, the chatter of his little sister infused him and squelched the terror in his sleep. No sirens screeched, the drawn-out screeches of the herons and the crack of the whip did not penetrate the small room.

On New Year's Eve his father did not forego the opportunity to celebrate his birthday again as usual. Aunt Molly was invited, and neighbors and friends joined in the celebration. Joseph and Hans sat with the girl on compulsory domestic service in the kitchen. They had hidden a bottle of wine from which they drank in secret. Joseph went out after midnight onto the cold hallway, onto his grandfather's path of pain. Somewhat later the domestic service girl followed him. She stood at the farthest corner of the hallway directly in front of him, took his hand and placed it through the open slit in her dress into a forest of coarse, curly hair. The young count came to Joseph's mind, and he was dismayed that he could not laugh like that, that something new, something experienced for the first time, could leave him mute.

He ran away. His brother had fallen asleep in the kitchen. His father's heavy deep voice echoed in the room.

In the morning the girl smiled at him, later she showed him love letters from two soldiers and photographs. She told him that one of them had already died in battle and one was missing in action. That was terribly upsetting and nerve-wracking. She showed him a gold ring, the wedding ring of her deceased mother. When she would hold the ring on a black piece of string over pictures, and the ring began to twirl, she would know that the person in the picture was still alive, but if the ring began to swing back and forth, the person was dead. In her spare time she went from house to house and earned a little money doing so.

During the course of the day Joseph ran into the headmaster. Joseph raised his hand, stretched it out far in front of him, in a Hitler salute. When the eyes of the headmaster reached him, be pulled his hand back and bent his fingers to a fist and put it down behind him. His eyes, which were blinded by the glance and the snow, had seen the pubic hair of the domestic service girl growing on the tips of his fingers. Then he hurried to the fir tree and tore down the signs battered by the snow. Behind it the fir tree had remained loyal to him.

71

At home his parents labeled the headmaster and several functionaries as typical Nazis. In the meantime Joseph had learned exactly who merely acquiesced and who counted as typical. If one disregarded the idiosyncrasies of speech, the personal ticks, the gait, the gestures, the ability to be friendly, only the plain, common picture remained. Without inhibition they were committed to hold their ideal with which they felt themselves united and which was therefore the sole truth for the absolute revelation. Their adjusted view prevented any other view, no matter whether it was feeble-minded or insightful. Time had stood still for them. They were numbed in the shock of the positive. Deep within they felt time had understood them, reflection found its happy end. Among themselves they were also united because they had their center in an authority whose existence resided outside of them. They were the mystics of their Führer, released to ascend from an evil history. They were living the renewal as the final event, as the rescuing order. Each one of them who abandoned the ideal crashed into the abyss. The outward gesture of their demeanor had long since become routine. Military life had invaded private life. They stood there like artificial objects, even in their breathing they were no longer themselves. Contrasted to all forms of re-formation throughout history, their celebrated association with evil was all that was actually new. They had transformed killing into a focal point of their culture. Killing was part of everything. If an Aryan child was rescued, they killed one of the hated race. Healthy children had need of the sick ones. The closely shorn skull was the presence of the head of death.

They were encountered this way everywhere, they stood behind the counters in the stores, in offices, in hospitals, in the classrooms, in front of their children. Their women had actually been born for them. Like cornflowers the women beamed in the seed of the model faithful, of the duty-conscious. Even though the women carried out their duty themselves in this world of unmerciful fathers, they often surpassed the men in their inflexibility. Although they all stood close to the Nordic tragedies and the decline was their stimulant, they behaved as if they had understood the Old Testament as little as *Mein Kampf*. Perhaps they hated the Jews because of the superiority of their ideal.

Joseph felt himself cast away from home as he traveled back to the city after the vacation. Unwillingly he had climbed into the overcrowded train. It smelled of groceries. Joseph stood crammed into a corner with soldiers. Later a member of the SS came along, a young, tall man with only one arm. The SS man opened his coat with his one hand. Under it he wore his medals. From his coat pocket he took a box of cigarettes of the kind that contained the pictures he collected. He asked Joseph to open the box. What Joseph feared secretly happened. On top lay picture 116; the SS man completed his collection. "Do you need the picture?" "Please," Joseph answered.

At the home he immediately pasted the picture into the album. The last empty space had disappeared. Picture was lined up next to picture so that it looked as if there were only one picture. Joseph hid the album in his locker.

After supper Joseph showed Johann the album. "You know," he said, "finally having something entirely complete is nice; it stays that way and doesn't change."

They stood in the darkness of the former church hall until they heard voices from all around. The cadets of their division were being looked for, they were supposed to assemble in the study hall. At the same time they heard piano music coming from a room beneath the cloak room, strange sounding rhythmical bits and pieces. Despite the order to assemble they followed the piano playing. Quietly they opened the door to the room. Students from the upper class were gathered around the black piano. Two cigarette lighters provided the light. The piano player was dressed in black and had long, dark hair covering his ears. With a high arched back he hunched over the keys. Joseph had heard similar music in movies, only it sounded more mellifluous and smoother there. "This way it's cruder," thought Joseph. When the nurse's friend noticed Joseph, he asked them to leave. They were to take their leave because they had been called up. What was taking place here was strictly prohibited, "but at the moment we don't belong to anyone."

The two of them rushed out of the door, the piano player had just stood up as they glanced back through the crack in the door. "Like a gypsy," said Joseph's friend. "He was playing jazz," the nurse's friend called after them.

In the study hall all the cadets were assembled. Paler than usual, Instructor Allemann was standing in front of the rows of desks. The off-white turtle-neck pullover reached to his chin, his hair was carefully parted, his hand hanged down limp, without quivering. "Go to your places," he commanded the two of them. The other cadets had hardly looked up. With eyes cast down they stared at the marred green desktops. "I'll repeat it for you two," said Allemann with an agitated voice, "one of the two Berger brothers, the older one, is dead." Joseph noticed that their places were empty. On the top of the desk a swastika had been drawn in chalk. "Misguided heroism," Allemann said.

They were not allowed to utter a word before going to bed. No one wanted to talk anyway; as if they were sitting together for the first time and no one knew anyone, they huddled together. Abruptly Allemann sent away the teacher's aide, who told stories of heroism every evening. No one took any notice. The music resounded in Joseph's ears, it hurt him, and soon it was so nebulous that only the piano player remained dancing before his eyes. He danced into the sameness destructively, tore and tattered the top of daily order and availability. He had crossed the border unnoticed like a person returning from the dead.

Allemann stayed in the sleeping hall for a long time until Joseph had fallen asleep, before he left.

Only at school did they find out what had happened. The older Berger brother had hidden a pistol in his coat pocket at home before his return to the home. It was one that belonged to his father, who he had just found out had been killed in Russia. On the way back he had boarded the same train on which Joseph had returned from home. He clutched the pistol in his coat pocket with his hand. As he was speaking with his brother, a shot was fired, dull as if it struck against an empty box. "Nothing, nothing," he had said, "we are going to need the pistol."

Only at the next station did he slump down and was dead in the middle of a sentence. "He wanted to be a werewolf," his brother said, "he wanted to avenge Father's death." "Why on the enemy?" asked the young count and was beaten black and blue.

73

"It's best," Joseph said to his friend, "if we tell each other what terrifies us like simple fairy tales. The less effort we make to use big words, and the less we suffer because we haven't learned to use them, the closer we will remain to the way which may at some point lead us in a different direction. Nothing is easier to speak than the terror. Nothing is as apparent, has so few sides. It is an exact matter, the most precise ordering of facts." They often enjoyed sensing the horror and experiencing the game as reality. "Since I have been in Graz, there has not been one single day," Joseph wrote to his mother, "when I have been the way I can often be at home, when I am with all of you or out of doors. I can't even write a composition in school, because I am not allowed even to have my own language here. The worst thing would be to say something differently than the way one wants to say it."

74

The most feared teacher was the drawing instructor. He sat outside on the podium and sketched like a frantic person. When he felt himself disturbed, he jumped up and stormed through the class. Within a few minutes he had checked the drawings and picked out his victims. Like a raging animal he punched and kicked the students who violated the order demanded of a particular color by infringing upon the border outlined on the drawing paper and invaded the enemy territory of the surrounding area. One of his grandfather's favorite flowers was the buttercup. That was precisely what Joseph had to copy with watercolors. Within the sketch of every flower that he drew was a chaos of color. The colors ran into one another, they attracted one another, swimming on the upper surface of excess water. "You will not survive the 1943-44 school year, that I swear in the name of the Führer."

The drawing instructor Karij had on high black boots; he wore pants similar to those of the SS. The jacket was longer than usual. His chubby face was red with anger or the passion to draw. The students traced the teacher's rage back to the fact that he was interrupted from drawing nudes during the class. Several of them had seen that there were naked women in the pictures, "dismembered women." Since now as before the young woman gym teacher Spinnhirn was at the school, they had no doubt that the drawing teacher had succeeded in conquering her. Whenever she did gymnastics with them, played handball, passed the medicine ball around in a circle, they saw the gym teacher through the imagination of their drawing teacher. His rage titillated their lack of shame with regard to the woman teacher. She was the offering, robbed of every secret. Her pubic area visible beneath her gym outfit was the tattered booty that belonged to them, she was condemned to fulfill their wishful fantasies. They dragged her into their reality, into the harsh light of release of passion, which the grownups enjoyed by virtue of their being able to kill freely with impunity.

75

During one of the nightly raids by the director and his teachers, just as they were standing naked next to their beds and showing their towels, the world finally struck back, something for which they had been prepared. Amidst the director's shouting, which was preceded by a message regarding Hitler's wishes about how he wanted his youth to be, burst the screech of an air-raid siren. The boys slipped into their socks, which had not yet been checked, put on their pajamas, their day clothes over them and stormed, not in panic, but in the practiced order into the cellar. On the way a dull droning already rolled above them and the bright, clicking sound of the anti-aircraft guns was heard. The lights in the cellar flickered and went out intermittently for minutes at a time. They sat wrapped in blankets. Nobody spoke a word, only the teachers paced back and forth, but sacrificed their position of superiority. Instructor Allemann sat in the middle of a row of students along the bare middle wall of the cellar. His fingers glided over a smallish book. He read without anyone being able to see what he was reading.

The next day the air raid on the city was the topic of conversation. "Did they speak English up there," one of the students asked the English teacher, "as they dropped the bombs on our city?" After classes Joseph walked past his Aunt Molly's house. When he saw that the house was unscathed and the shade of the one window tightly drawn, he hurried on to Aunt Elly's. In front of the house he met his uncle, who took him inside. In the large parlor stood the piano with the sheet music strewn all over it and the metronome. His uncle asked him whether he really did not want to take violin lessons with him as had been agreed upon with his mother. Joseph did not dare say no. The uncle fetched a violin case wrapped in a cloth. "This is one of your grandfather's violins," he said, "you can have one of them. Since all he does now is philosophize and sees the world declining, he has given up playing the violin and has replaced it with the organ." He handed Joseph the violin, positioned it under his chin, and pressed the neck of the violin into Joseph's cramped palm. Then he had to take the bow in his fingers and lay it on the strings. The uncle took his violin and slowly drew the bow across one of the strings, as the deep sound wafted softly through the room. Joseph was supposed to do the same, but as soon as he started to draw the bow, the violin slipped to the left as if one arm were avoiding the other. "Your little brain is not working," said his uncle. "It was also the same with playing the piano; your fingers imitated one another and couldn't do anything independently."

Then his uncle played a violin solo for him and a piece on the piano that he had composed himself. On the shelves next to the piano stood two thick music scores bound in red. When Joseph looked over, his uncle said to him, "Yes, my opera, after the war it will certainly be performed." Later he asked, "Does Grandfather still deliver his speeches to you?" "He doesn't believe in victory," answered Joseph. "We are already victorious."

Suddenly standing in the room, Aunt Elly interrupted the uncle. "You know those are artists' thoughts," she said. "It would be better if your uncle would compose rather than trivialize music in front of fellow comrades. Do you want to eat with us?" "I've eaten," the uncle suddenly screamed excitedly and bolted out the door. Joseph said goodbye, his aunt advised him to learn more. "You know, English."

76

A few days before his name day Joseph took sick. How long had he had to wait for this fever; he thought that his friendship with the nurse's friend would have endeared him to her. He was assigned the last free bed. The patients were lying there in a row of ten, and the nurse was rather perturbed when Allemann brought him into the room. "You with your red urine," she said.

The doctor came within a few hours. The director and Instructor Allemann accompanied him. Joseph knew the doctor. He was Aunt Elly's brother-in-law, a quiet physician who inspired trust and had often excised the boils on Joseph's neck with his large handsome hands. Just as he approached Joseph's bed, the director, glancing at the beautiful nurse, said to the doctor, "There's nothing wrong with any of them;

they're sick from masturbating, we haven't been able to weed that out yet." Joseph stared at Instructor Allemann, as if he might ameliorate Joseph's shame in front of the doctor. It was as if the whole family were standing in front of him in the person of the doctor. As if he had been discovered and simultaneously betrayed the family, Joseph lay there, and he was also disconcerted because Instructor Allemann looked away. Then the director whispered into the doctor's ear who seemed to pass along the secret to the nurse. Joseph heard how the nurse said to the doctor with a smile, "And I'm sharing the rooms with these ten teenagers."

Later on no one said a word. For the first time it was as if the conversations among them were almost stifled. Like strangers they lay in the infirmary, and each of them seemed only to know one person, the nurse. Instructor Allemann came to visit him and a second student from his division in the morning and in the afternoon. Most of the time Instructor Allemann talked with the other boy. Not a word came to Joseph that he could nave uttered. As at home, he let himself be driven out to the pond, for the first time he longed to have the herons nearby. Outside the sky was springlike, the air was clear, the roofs of the houses glistened. At home the first flowers would already be blooming, as always.

77

On the morning of Joseph's name day his father suddenly showed up on his motorcycle. He brought Joseph a large package with groceries. His father was in a hurry. He told him only that the fish had been stocked. There were many soldiers in the village again. An officer was living in his grandfather's room.

During his free time—they usually had an hour to go out—Joseph wanted to celebrate his name day secretly with the bread, the paté, the dried ham, and sausages. As they were preparing to celebrate, the sirens began to howl. Undetected, they left the home and ran to the Schlossberg.

They went into the middle of the mountain, cowered in a corner, and ate their meal of celebration without speaking. They edged closer together when the news spread like wildfire that wave after wave of planes was attacking the city. Within the mountain none of it could be heard. Their bodies disappeared in the rock, they delivered up the one who had condemned them to tremble here. They pressed their way out through the stone, through the opening of the sky that extended down to the earth, from which death fell; they were untouched by it there, where what was "inside" drew them. Joseph sat at home beneath the radio, ate the yellow pudding; on the bench next to him stood his parents, who pressed their ears to the loudspeaker and heard the "black transmitter." What his parents themselves had once desired now dawned as a surprise attack. "It's a comfort," said the father, "to lose one's ego. The guilt terrifies me, when again after the war other machines will calculate the guilt."

After the all-clear signal it took them over a half an hour to get back to daylight. The people in front of them were scurrying about in all directions. They saw the home unscathed in front of them. There it did not seem to have occurred to anyone that they were not in the cellar. After an hour the director came, had them enter the courtyard, divided them into groups, and designated a group leader. The groups were assigned to different streets that had been destroyed to help with the cleanup effort. For the first time they witnessed the destruction, the transformation of a familiar sight into a myriad of brick, wood, and smashed possessions. Joseph heard one of the shocked persons affected by the attack say despairingly to other people standing around, "This is how it must once have been within the masters who got us in trouble. Everything all around can be gone, it's all the same to them, because they still have their ideals."

They dragged brick and pieces of walls well into the night, uncovered tracks, supported collapsed panels of signs, and cleaned the signs of dirt and dust. While they were working, men in Party uniforms came along, clicking their heels and saluting, they again cast the net of order over the ruins. It was actually as if those standing around felt comforted and protected.

On the way back to the home they saw that bombs had also fallen near the home. The building with the stationery store had disappeared and, as they discovered, the apprehensive woman paper dealer was dead. They ran off quickly to the bordello. There the soldiers were processing in and out as usual. During the night Joseph stretched out his arm from the bed and touched the fingertips of his friend Johann.

78

Because the events snowballed day by day and it became part of the daily day and night game to spread reports or to hinder their spread, the confusion grew. But it was always quickly cast aside, as the arms of truth knew how to restore clarity quickly. Nothing produces more truth and unanimity than fear. It does not isolate but brings together. In order not to sacrifice any secret, to betray no voice from the abyss, they followed the one voice. Fear saw to it that a certain joy was maintained. "We are one people and cannot live without a spirit ruling over us; we have no brains, a spirit has us, no matter whether we are philosophers or vintners in the vineyard," his father's father once said. "The spirit functions, it need not be concerned that it is not being obeyed. The most we will lose is the war, but for the time being no enemy will conquer this spirit. Since the spirit is no longer God, it is especially bad. Save me, you blossoming apple trees and vineyards."

The terror that ran rampant made use of the resolve to confront it as unavoidable death; one did not take it seriously, one believed himself able to divert it or negotiate with it. The idea was not allowed to decay; it was not allowed to be turned into smoked meat. "Earlier we join with the enemy and lead him over to where he doesn't matter to us, in order to transform ourselves, away from ourselves, again into something generic."

On free afternoons on the weekends they swept through the city. Houses in front of which Joseph had once stood had disappeared, the pavement torn up. The destruction passed over the holes in the walls, the beams, the people, as if it standardized their individual fates. They went to soccer games. When one of the city's two favorite teams played against the SS team, the mood almost turned treasonous and revealed that the enthusiastic hearts had often followed only the power of words to convince. They fought on the soccer field, they ran around aimlessly and were happier about a condom found behind the city park bench than about the reports that were supposed to be indications of a positive turning point in the war. When they stretched a condom over their fingers, only the most obstinate among them forgot that they had become defenseless in facing the enemy. The hunchbacked school superintendent had remained as he was. The bad gymnast remained as despised as ever. The confusion aided those who maintained the order. They made one color out of many. They were the masters of the twilight, evil offers no resistance when it is administered, it lives itself out and accepts gladly what is the same and held in common.

Next to the paper dealer's destroyed house was a fish store. The smell of fish attracted them, it reminded them of themselves, of the deprivation of having warm water only once a week. "Woman is a fish," the mathematics teacher with the leg infirmity had said, and the old, hook-nosed Latin teacher, who used language to discipline, as if this language had never been spoken by a living human being, extolled the healthy body.

They bought the cheapest fish sandwiches. Right in the middle of the slice of onion was a piece of herring. The sticky onion rings slipped over their fingers as they ate and then smelled even more like fish than the fish. As they ate, they sat near the market booths under the chestnut trees. At the home they did not wash their hands. They smelled their hands until late into the night as if another life were sticking to them, as if they had run away from having to obey and were free, free like they were in reaching for their genitals or for the penis of another.

The director and the teachers suffocated from the repetition, they were condemned to not being able to say anything else. They had no more triumphs or examples, they had a hard time switching from the joy of the victors to the joy of the defenders. Their reality games, their fanaticism turned into shadow games. They themselves seemed to be surprised that they had more ardent supporters than before, adults and children, those ready to die and the simple-minded. They still lived beyond the contradiction. The opposing voice was hotter, rootless, at best alive in the confusion of individuals, who were for them sick and destructible, they provided only a bad example for a good purpose. Sometimes Joseph believed one had let them lie together in the beds in order to promote community, the preparedness for death, the silence, the acceptance, the useful, realizable guilt.

79

On the day of the unsuccessful assassination attempt on the Führer, Joseph was at his parents'. They were sitting outside the entrance to the house, in the middle of them was the father's hunting dog. Then a Hitler Youth leader came along on a bicycle, churned up dust as he braked, and said: "They tried to murder the Führer." They remained silent and were scared to death that they were even able to keep silent. They did not hide their own "political" opinion; they had perhaps unlearned having their own. Their possessions that they had buried months ago were the non-consoling form of their counteropinion. It was deep enough beneath the earth so that one could equate them with the dead.

Hesitatingly they took their leave of one another when the school year ended. They had gotten to know each other well; they had their hiding places and trusted one another. They wanted to see each other again; the contradictions bound them together, no teacher or instructor had elicited such enthusiasm for them that he could have drawn them to him. Allemann was closer to them, he left them more perplexed than the other teachers.

In the village things were topsy-turvy. The castle in the park was a meeting point for the officer staff. The officers liked to recline on the modern furniture. Nobody welcomed this second quartering with the enthusiasm that practically produced a feeling of brotherhood during the first one. The mass death of the first ones who were quartered evoked shyness in the face of those consecrated for death in the second. "How can they be so happy?" his mother asked. It was a Bavarian division. Those in charge of the central kitchen located in the yard of the parents' house were masters of organization. At least for the staff and those quartered in the village there were genuine peace banquets. When they moved out again in the middle of the summer, there were no good-byes. Even the political functionaries were happy about it. Now they were in control again. The soldiers had disrupted their order, and besides that they were crown witnesses of the military situation. People did not like to see them, just as little as they did the increasing number of furloughed local soldiers from families in the village.

Towards the end of the vacation his father received orders to report. On the last Sunday he took Joseph and Hans duck hunting. From the time they were small, both had been excellent drivers. Two officers were among the hunting guests. Joseph's father had positioned them in such a way that the majority of the ducks flew towards them. After the hunt it was as if they had been dulled from shooting. While the hunters went with the officers for the last drive, Joseph and Hans searched for mushrooms. They had just come back to the inn as the officers were climbing into their car. "Who did you pick those for?" asked one of the officers. "For our father," said Hans. "You can take joy in your children," the officer called to the father, "I would die for mushrooms," and drove off in the car. In the evening their mother told both of them that one of the officers was a dentist and would be in charge of the call-up the next day.

During the night Hans woke up Joseph. "The sun will be rising soon. Let's go pick mushrooms in the woods so that the officer dies," he said to Joseph. Before it got fully light, they had already gathered a basket of fresh mushrooms. A quarter of an hour before the call-up they surprised the officer at breakfast in the inn and gave him the mushrooms. He looked at them in amazement. "You said you would die for the mushrooms," said Hans. In the fresh morning breeze they rode home, the meadows were smooth after the second mowing and appeared larger than usual. The alder trees around them created quiet areas, as if cut out of the narrowing space. They told their parents that they had been in the park, at their favorite places for the last time.

81

"They have condemned you to be something you are not," said Maria Szmaragovska. Joseph was around her a lot during the summer vacation. Daily he fetched the milk from the cow stalls in the farm building. Maria Szmaragovska also helped with the milking. She had gotten heavy. "It became unbearable for me to stay the same."

The Russian prisoners of war were more fearful and shy than before. The tools with which they crafted their jewelry had disappeared. Those who had been torn from their world and robbed of their homeland feared having to move to another place. "You have your district," so it was said, and they were compelled to go along. They had turned into empty people for whom someone was perhaps waiting, but no longer the Volk. They were used up and interchangeable with thousands of others; they were poorer for the fact that their peoples were victorious all around.

Where would they find a place for them to establish roots again? Their purpose in life was for the time being to escape death. They were who they were in the wrong place, where it made least sense. With every day the war went on, their homeland came closer, it crept nearer, promised freedom. The homeland of the ones they obeyed became more constricted. They were imprisoned in another way.

82

Joseph stood in front of the cross at the end of the tree-lined walk. What greeted him was the earth beneath his feet and the smell from the fields. Deep silence was all around. The yellow scull place of the pumpkin patches glistened; the dried out corn leaves stood out starkly, the trail of red bugs ran across to the tree-lined walk. Joseph's desire to go from flower to flower, to look from leaf to leaf, from split bark to split bark, had in the truest sense of the word diminished. The colored leaves of the front of trees formed a surface on which the colors danced as they changed, as if the drawing teacher's border surrounded them. People and nature made themselves scarce, they did not make their presence known.

The tree-lined path was exit and entrance. The one who searched for the names of things, for the "forms of things," Joseph, read the writing on the trees. The trees had gotten larger, the tree-lined walk older, the linden trees had disappeared, the same red of the beetles shone. The "silent world" had become more silent, as if this were happiness. The seeker of things asks: "What was that?" Was it that which still is? Is it in the heads? There are no heads. Who speaks the words? Remembrance is without power, what is terrifying deserves no story and no neutrality of understanding.

Joseph walked back down the path. The underbrush of the clearing where the children had discovered themselves and had occupied themselves as foreign lands, had gotten higher; grass and flowers grew tall.

In the clearing Joseph would be able to experience moments of returning to the world, the release and soothing exhaustion of the reencounter, the leap from the release of the seed to the embrace of a liberating calm. Where the boys had sat, stood parasols, mushrooms with large caps. The beech, ash, and oak trees persevered above those absent. Joseph placed himself like the young count in the middle of the clearing, as if he could drive the whole pretense of the Movement from his body and from the world by trying to create freedom for himself. It crawled up his back and all around him the colors brightened, but then he knelt down and cried. He felt powerless with his desires. He could have imagined Allemann being there, taking part in the attempt to say goodbye, silently having a voice.

83

On the day before Joseph was taken to the train with his brother, his parents' home was seized "provisionally" by the SS. With an ax they had broken down the door and quartered themselves. The occupiers permitted the family to take along the most important things. They moved into the inn in the village, with people to whom love of their fellow man was a given and nothing was asked in return.

Joseph observed the SS men drinking beer in the inn. With a beer coaster in front of his eyes, he cut out the heads from his field of vision. He stared at them and waited until they got up as human heads from being condemned to their uniforms. The faces repeated the stupidity all around, the murdering that belonged to their bodies. The urge to do away with aliens lay like a rash on their faces. They sat there and waited for the messengers because they had recognized correctly that they were not there for any other reason.

For the first time Joseph left his place of residence as one that was no longer familiar to him. The last night before the departure he lay awake in a strange room with strange photographs. He heard sirens coming from the market and soon thereafter the window panes rattled from the bombing squadrons. The house became restless. The animals in the stall pawed.

Having his brother sitting next to him in the train eased the departure and lessened the anxiety. Would his brother find out where the older cadets were going? Joseph did not dare tell Hans about it. It was impossible for him. He was ashamed for his brother, and in the silence what had survived over the three years expanded into listless awakening.

But Hans soon learned what the home was all about. The all-encompassing destruction encircled the home. The great, often practiced preparation for the whole, the world order, shrunk together as house orders. In this way the future which was being lost became a small present, the victory they hoped for, the final victory, poisoned them with the expectation of the end. When they returned from vacation, a majority of the houses were covered with camouflage. To the eye of the enemy the visible was made invisible, what was was not supposed to be. Everyone began to camouflage himself, whether he remained silent or continued to be jubilant, whether he believed in the weapon of recompense or hoped a turn would come from the Japanese. Camouflaged, the city stuck its head in the sand.

In the home it was only Allemann who stayed the same. He had not increased anything, relaxed anything, or discarded anything; he continued to have his room guarded and directed the more infrequent evening showers. He stood in front of their beds, gazed without rage, without pitting one against the other, before he turned off the light and walked away limping, as if it were difficult for him to have to go back to his room. Only then did it occur to them that he was a part of their nights, in which he was not permitted to take part, when the no longer unsurprising checks tore them from their sleep. They had also become more careful. The way inward opened itself up. Being cautious and secretive took the upper hand. The clear commandments and the one will that encircled and devoured them lost its effectiveness. They sensed that Instructor Allemann had been right. He had come without threat; in the middle of this manufactured, calculated, incited coldness he was the illusion of the other standing on the side, a remnant, an illness not fully cured. Appearances toyed with him, he assumed the look in order to remain invisible; he did not use himself up with exaggerated appearances like the others.

84

During a free hour a few days after a fierce bomb attack, while the cadets were playing soccer with cans of food in the yard, reading, or comparing and exchanging pieces of bomb shrapnel, the bell to assemble rang. During the seemingly incessant ringing, the teachers shouted, "Line up, line up!" In a few minutes they were standing in rows of four, lined up perfectly and simultaneously without a clue, and guessed that there would again be a final call-up.

On the wall of the low factory building, which bordered one part of the yard to the west, the kitchen girls sat peeling potatoes. Falling leaves from the chestnut trees danced in the air. Tearing the door to the courtyard wide open, the director of the home appeared in uniform. He briefly looked for the right place to stand, quickly found it and shouted, although everyone was standing there agape and the girls stopped peeling the potatoes, "Attention, we now have him, the one who has defiled you and has caused this mess that has come to our attention. It is Instructor Dr. Allemann. He has already been arrested." Right then a small door opened that led into an annex of the home. Two policemen in civilian clothing, who had come along the wall of the house to the door through which the director had entered, were leading the handcuffed teacher. Allemann walked no differently than usual; his face remained unchanged. Later on some thought he had been laughing.

The director immediately put an end to the helplessness and wild outbreak of curiosity. He herded them into the courtyard for exercises. Intermittently when they again had to stand at attention and look straight ahead, he screamed, “These foolish deeds are now over, now you belong to us.” When they went back to the home, the kitchen girls had disappeared, the nurse had come in order to care for several of them who had hurt themselves. Joseph regretted not having an injury, nothing would have benefited him more at the moment. His brother Hans stood in front of Instructor Siegmund and cried.

In the evening and while the boys were preparing for bed, the strictest silence was in effect. Two teachers walked continually through the sleeping halls and also checked the two washrooms. Then they turned the light off and left the door to the hall open. There was complete silence.

They deceived themselves by thinking they would receive more information at school. Only in the evening was part of the puzzle solved. They found out that the parents of the cadets from Allemann’s group had been apprised of everything. After that no talking was allowed again.

On the next day after lunch his father stood with the other parents, mostly mothers, in front of the dining hall. “We wouldn’t have imagined that,” he said to Joseph. “What?” replied Joseph. The parents followed the director and the teachers to the office. The cadets assembled in the study hall; after an hour Instructor Siegmund appeared and informed them that the parents had been made privy to the secret and were appropriately scandalized. For certain reasons the director had avoided talking with them even now. The parents had just left the home.

A little while later another teacher brought the first cadet to the director’s office. When he came back looking pale, he called out the name of another boy and the process continued this way until Joseph too was called.

In the office behind the wide desk to the left and the right of the director sat the two men who had led Allemann off in handcuffs. One was holding a sheet of paper in his hand. "In the file on Instructor Allemann it says that you are unreliable, that your trust can be won quickly, but that it is not clear whether or not you would keep your promises. Did Herr Allemann ever molest you indecently?" "No." "Did you ever hear him say in the sleeping hall, 'Anyone who doesn't masturbate, is not a German youth?'" "Yes." "You can go."

The last five from the group were summoned at the same time. They found out nothing from these five the next day. The others reported exactly what they had been asked. Above all the ones with the condoms from the adjoining hall had to describe the events in complete detail, as the criminal officers prompted them with the appropriate words, in order to facilitate the confessions. It occurred to them that no one was asked with whom he had been in bed.

Right after this event a change took place in them. It came about by itself. Their bond and search for protection, their freedom and the self-preservation that came over them in the secret that was open and yet hidden from them had been swept away with Allemann. The illusion was destroyed, the last remnant had turned to truth. They themselves now suddenly felt the urge to betray Allemann. They took their revenge on him, without actually knowing how he had destroyed their world, which was joined to him. In doing so, they reconstructed his rambling sentences and his smiling into accusations. He was the fitting motive to be ordinary with good reason. All of a sudden the teachers seemed mellow to all of them, and the teachers also confirmed when they did not avoid emphasizing that from now on things were heading in only one direction. The glory of the successes and victories that ran aground because of an excess of power turned into the glory of the end and of the reversal emerging out of it.

With enthusiasm the cadets who were a year older obeyed the necessity of this duty by taking part in the erecting of the eastern wall. They were celebrated when they left the school and home. Smiling, they entered the river that carried them away. Many cursed having been born too late. They had to wait before belonging entirely to the Party; they wanted to follow its power. What the teachers called the State was foreign to them. The Party was the characteristic of the race, with the spade they marched toward the foxholes and embankments of their ancestors. They were sent out to repeat the eternal offering of the border, and the Reich seemed to consist solely of borders. Their shovels and the burying of the seed, their power to defend and their will to receive deepened the myth of that which always remained the same. "Arise, Styrians, to your work! If we are not unfaithful to the Führer and to ourselves, the victory at the end of our struggle will surely come to pass."

In the sleeping hall many beds were empty; hands groped half asleep into the void. Instructor Siegmund replaced Allemann's limping gait with the bloody tracks of forceful steps. "If it were not a disgrace to throw the soap at you, I would do it every second you do not act as if you are the Volk's conscripts. Cleanse yourselves with the extraction of filth; the soap has no value as a weapon."

85

On November 1 Joseph went to school with his brother, his friend Johann, and another cadet named Bergmann, who was Joseph's boxing partner. Right in front of the school building Joseph said that he was accompanying his brother to an X-ray technician. He was scheduled for a checkup there because of his cough. They came back to class two hours later with a negative diagnosis. It was already break time. They went up the stairs to the second floor. Half way up Joseph met the woman English teacher. Her lipstick was pale in several places, in one spot it was smeared towards her chin. "You skipped my class, I'll be attending the one after the next, and then I will deal with you. In the meantime I'll get your student profile, which will complete the picture." As she uttered these words in her raging High German, Joseph observed that her fingertips were covered with white and red chalk. The ring with the glittering stone was turned inward as if ready to help tear open his face.

"The Führer needs you," the Latin teacher said during the following class, "I need your vocabulary notebooks." They said of him that he was a socialist who preferred speaking Latin instead of German. "Soon you will not be learning Latin any longer," he said, "I've been recruited to the Volkssturm."

A little bit later the siren rescued Joseph from the impending torture by the English teacher. The siren knocked the English teacher's ring and the headmaster's words out of commission. Joseph looked for his brother, and then they left the school together the same way they had come. Joining them was only the student Strauss, a farmer's son, whom they once had to beat up because he had appropriated a better reader. They were fond of him because of his blue lady's coat with the large white mother-of-pearl buttons. He wore it because his mother had no money to buy him a more suitable one. Strauss ran on ahead of them. As if he were their mother, they followed him to the Schlossberg tunnels across from the home, although they were not very far from the home.

Since they were accustomed to spending All Saints' Day remembering the dead and standing at the cemetery in the November light, they did not enter far into the protective grave of the inner mountain. Only a few meters from the entrance they squatted on their drawing pads and school bags in a freshly dynamited side tunnel. They thought that on this day the memory of death would compel the will to kill. "Where is Allemann?" asked Strauss. "With those who know more about him," answered Johann.

From their hiding place they suddenly heard the sounds of engines coming and going and of flak grenades exploding. In the calm that followed they experienced a greater fear than before. For the first time they admitted that they were afraid. They took their drawing pads and placed them over their heads. Above them were loose pieces of rock. "We've got to get out of here," said Joseph's friend. They jumped up and went back to the main tunnel. A beam of light coming from the entrance was shining so brightly and enticingly as if it could extinguish the fear on its own accord. They were so enthralled by it that they ran out of the tunnel. The home stood there camouflaged. For the first time Joseph believed it would be better to be there than where he was. As they thought about whether they should bolt to reach the home, a surging din came in their direction, explosions and the roar of planes forced them back into the tunnels. Just as they disappeared inside, they thought the mountain over them was crashing down. Pieces of rock struck their drawing pads, dust flew up, and the light faded. After a few seconds a sudden calm overcame them as if they were buried beneath it. Just as quickly a fit of screaming followed the calm. With their drawing pads and book bags under their arms as if they had allowed duty to become part of their bodies, they ran out. The light outside choked with dust, and when the dust unveiled a niche, they saw that there was a large section of the home in which dark patterns raged. Like the apparition of a saint, a dark cloud arched over it. Without looking at one another, they dashed off in unison. Right beyond the power station in whose water supply canal the foreign worker had lain dead, several bomb craters gaped. Fear of death and the urge to salvage some mementos simultaneously determined their action. They slid into the bomb crater because gigantic bomb shrapnel was lying there, and Joseph's brother, who had discovered the biggest piece, screamed when he grabbed it because it was still red hot. Then they ran across the bridge over the river. Right in the middle Strauss bent over the railing and, almost ceremoniously, hurled his school supplies into the river. Notebooks and textbooks fluttered down and were swept off in the raging water. When Strauss was finished, Joseph and his brother did the same, but without his sense of ceremony, because a new wave of bombs was raining over the city. Joseph hovered in a furrow on the other side of the river. He saw the rock in front of him from which he had fallen down right in front of the SS man's exposed genitals.

Men from the fire department and the air-raid squadron chased them away grumblingly. Over the upturned fence of the yard they climbed back to the "village" with which they had come into contact a thousand times with their bodies condemned to "up and down."

Just as they returned, the cadets were coming from the cellar; dust-covered, they crawled out amidst the rubble, several were grinning already as if they had vanquished the enemy because they were not dead. The director of the home put an end to the confusion. With his uniform dust-covered and his face beet-red, he triumphed over the catastrophe. The home was destroyed, floors were standing only to the left and the right of the main section. The one-time chapel with the wardrobes was destroyed; Joseph's album, bacon, and bread had disappeared. In a split second they stood there in the old formation, and as if nothing had happened, they had to sound off and confirm that no one was missing. The nurse stood by helplessly with bandages. Instructor Siegmund was wearing a white bandage at which the director glared in contempt. The director repeated that everyone was there and that the enemy had achieved no result with them, as if they had been the enemy's sole target.

Then they were given the command to put out the fires flaring up in the cloth factory next to the home. Joseph poured buckets of water over smoking bales of material; the young count jumped from one bale to the other and imagined a time bomb in every indentation. Again it was necessary to protect themselves. The Führer had steeled them. Imperiously and ferociously they carried the buckets against the resistance of the fire. They relished the biting smoke. They had no time for the gentle clouds in the carefree sky. Animals of prey jumped over the burned sites. In jumping, their beauty was fulfilled; they jumped over the measuring tape of their teacher Spinnhirn. They became more athletic with the effort. The slaves were transformed into free men, water-pouring, fire-extinguishing. They were led back over the bales of material to true nature. In the rubble the director saw those following orders as the new generation. The spirit was the fire that burns. Extinguishing it, they had the knowledge behind them, the terror of the matter. It is corrupting the youth. Willingly the beating of the fire subdued the flames, the scandal of the firebombs. The fear of death was active in the rubble. Heroically one took the brick from the whole of the crumbled wall that, having fallen, became measure and midpoint of the overturned world. God is the mortar. Human beings had decided to throw their school "things" into the river. Bodies became freer for death, the masculine maturity. The ruins presented the battle order for the being or non-being of the Volk. Blackened with soot, trembling in the face of the time bombs imagined by the count, they found their way back again to the rows of four. Along the way Joseph discovered the shreds of his album.

"It is a victory that we are whole," shouted the director and, as if alongside this language of this man another language was actually speakable, someone shouted, "Where are you all, where are you?"

Then Joseph's father appeared. He stood on the heap of rubble between the crumbled roof rafters. He was wearing Lederhosen that reached over the knee, gray socks, and his deerskin coat with its silver sheen. He appeared in the flesh, took his sons, and paid no attention to the director as he called out his orders. "You go today with Johann to Aunt Molly, Hans is going home with me. A truck will bring you home in the morning." As the father went off with Hans, Johann said, "This is the way we are victorious."

86

The father had appeared; the fear that something bad might happen to his sons was overcome. He stood there crying. In his sons his life was replicated. They had prevented his being called up with the mushrooms they picked as the sun was rising, but they never told the father. Often it sufficed to just be a son. The father's appearance at the ruins loomed so large that it overshadowed what had taken place. The appearance, not their review, became the measure of things.

It was already dark when they arrived at Aunt Molly's. On the way there they passed by the house of Aunt Elly and their uncle. They heard him at the piano; relieved, they followed the devastated streets. There was still no light when Joseph and his friend went to bed at Aunt Molly's. They slept in a small room rented out by the aunt. The renter had been killed that day in the bombing.

Joseph and his friend embraced; they fended off the memory of the dead man, whose pajamas were still under the bed pillow. After midnight the sirens howled their warning signal. They squeezed their hands together. Each hand was its own messenger. What it was lacking was the time of arrival.

In the morning the aunt came to their room with the newspaper and read aloud to them that Instructor Allemann had been sentenced to death by beheading for seducing an "entire home." They grabbed the newspaper from the aunt's hands. "After every finality comes another one," she said.

After breakfast they went their separate ways. Joseph's friend went to his relatives, Joseph to the truck. He sat down on the bed of the truck and left the city with his head hanging down.

Far away from the city on the open country road, while the driver was filling up with gas, Joseph thought of Allemann's head and his swinging arm. It struck the hole through which Joseph returned home, and Joseph saw the hollow in the fir tree that wanted to reemerge from it.

The truck brought him to the inn. The path with the linden trees had turned brown; the leaves had already fallen from some of the trees. The air-raid station was hidden by corn stalks, which were still standing. He got out of the truck in front of the inn. Joseph returned with only what he had on his body. Sobbing, his mother ran toward him; the innkeeper's wife quickly made an omelet with bacon and placed a large glass of hard cider in front of him. "He needs that." Later his father arrived with his brother. He too brought the newspaper with the verdict on Allemann.

In the guest room the newspaper was passed around. When they looked at Joseph and questioned him, he had the feeling they thought he had come back because of the evil-doer Allemann. "He should have been in a concentration camp long ago."

Towards evening Joseph went to the cross and then down the tree-lined walk to where they lived. Just as he entered the yard, and looked up to the bay window, the upper body of an SS man protruded from the window in which he had last seen his grandfather alive. "Do you know the people who live here?" he shouted at Joseph. Joseph said yes. "Tell them that we will be gone in an hour." Joseph hurried back to the inn.

On the next day they had reestablished the old order, even Vergely's picture was hanging in its place. Joseph's parents permitted him to sleep in his grandfather's room. "Allemann has wiped out my fear of death," he said to Hans.

Several days later there was a knock at the door during lunch; the nurse's friend was there in uniform.

He stayed until evening. By the dam of an empty fish pond they sat down on the trunk of an overturned oak. On the way the friend told of his war experiences. He was on furlough recuperating from jaundice. Only after Joseph tried to tell him about Allemann and the destruction of the home, did he say, “I know more about it than you.” Allemann had bound the five from his section closely to him. These five had had the power to find him. He demanded that they, his circle, learn his secret code and silence. He read poems to them. As he read, he stood up and sat down at the raised head of the bed. One of the five had to spread out a large white handkerchief on the bed, Allemann took his excited member in his hand and let the semen flow onto the handkerchief after taking a deep breath. “I wanted passion to return to the hardened faces of the boys,” he said before the judge, “I never touched them, only watched.” This business with the German boy and that the five had betrayed him had cost him his head.

The nurse had been summoned as a witness. She too recounted that the five had confirmed that Allemann was guilty of everything. Without introducing any proof, the court permitted the five to speak the alleged truth.

On the way home after his friend had taken leave of him, Joseph went to the fir tree. With his pocket knife he scratched out the hole and shouted into it, “I’m back.” Allemann’s image emerged out of the turmoil.

Allemann had prevented the first ones from remaining first. The children in the park, the soldier at the swimming pool, the cadets in the neighboring sleeping hall already repeated Allemann’s signs. Allemann’s defeat was Allemann’s victory. He had escaped the authority of the one truth and had left behind the traces to the other way.

87

“Out of many things the opposite now arises,” said the grandfather upon leaving. On a sunny December day he suddenly stood in the kitchen. “My last visit,” he said, “I’m disappearing with the Reich. I still have the strength to make my way home to the volcanic earth, it’s better without hope, the predictions are already answered.” As he walked down the staircase, he called back a few times, “The offensive in the

Ardennes that has just begun is already lost, what will come is already past. The present is in hiding."

88

Without regard for the strict regulations, animals were slaughtered at Christmas. We need strength, the men of the Volkssturm said. With their short Italian guns on their backs, they set up facilities for roadblocks and dug out trenches running the perimeter to defend against tanks. Through the village the smell of roasts wafted. The headmaster had to close the school. He guarded foreign workers, who were digging out new positions behind the southeast wall. "We are pressing forward toward the final victory." The school was no longer the school, Maria Szmaragovska's kitchen became a gathering place for the Volkssturm and the antitank grenade launchers. Although the Poles were still living and working in the farm building, Maria Szmaragovska was taken away at the same time with the captured Russians. A forest guard recounted he had seen them disappear in the forest days later at dusk. On New Year's Eve they heard on the radio that Hitler had ordered the counteroffensive in the West. Aunt Molly had just arrived and heard the news with concern, because her son and her husband were in this front pincer. A few days later she found out that on the day of the attack her son, of whom and of whose future she still spoke proudly, had been shot down with the pilot, and her husband, the uncle with the early warning that was heard too late, had been taken prisoner. The new year seemed like the reverse of the year of jubilation. The Movement did an about-face and was frozen in what had remained the same from the beginning, that the truth lay off in the future, in the will to not discard this truth.

"The truth had turned into the Party."

With the gray of morning Joseph saw the headmaster trudging through the snow and followed by his wife draped in black. He too came into the yard and up the staircase into the hallway. Without asking whether he were allowed to, he walked to the end of the hallway and back, first past Joseph, as if he did not notice him, then he remained standing and said, "What are you doing here, weren't you one of the instructor's boys?" "I'm looking at the cooked head of the pig," replied Joseph and removed the cover from the large pot. The pig's head, in whose eyes orange carrots were sticking, stared at the headmaster, who again went out and down the stairs, shouting, "I'm going to have it impounded." Joseph watched him leave and was again thankful to him because he was the reason that his father had struck him. At lunch they ate the head, several guests from the evening were invited. They didn't stop eating until the bare skull had no meat left on it. Teeth and eye sockets showed signs of having been devoured and grabbed at. "Now there is nothing more in the head," said the father, "only what is the hardest has remained."

"What are we going to do with ourselves?" asked the mother. "Our sense of conviction has vanished. Who will we say we were?" "Finally that which they intended us to be," a guest continued. "But now as before we are what we are," interjected another. "Was not that which they intended for us, also in us?" "In us?" asked the father and struck the silver fork on the bony skull of the pig.

89

In the weeks that followed the sky was saturated with bomber squadrons flying over. Death fell over the city. It struck into the abyss of this city, in which only one version of love showed Joseph what human beings are. From the city came the summons to give one's all; they let out the cry, through self-destruction they wanted to preserve a self that never was. The preservers showed up at Joseph's village as well. With their whips they lashed out around them with slogans and threats. Like dead men who had believed they had only been dreaming that they were dead, they spread the terror of continuing to live. They had deserters hanged at the market place, for three days the dead swayed back and forth and were robbed at night of their clothing. There was not one repentant person, not one, who dared to repent. They had never learned to discard the truth and to say they had gone astray. They confused the ability to persevere until the hour promised them arrived with steadfastness and the guise of character. They had never been allowed to live, therefore they lived for this actual false life. They let themselves be freed from the non-essential in order to be free for the brutality of necessity.

Undaunted, spring led its arrival and blossoming back to where it had its place. On a moonlit night one of the soldiers from the air guard looked away from the sky to the field and noticed some movement there. When he, directed back from the heavens to the danger of the earth, fired several times, three people stood up and surrendered, two men and a woman, Russians, who had jumped out of an airplane. They had gotten into the wrong territory. "The people from the East don't know their geography," the headmaster said, as he was standing guard in front of the morgue in which the three were held prisoner before they were executed. He believed that people arrived at an appropriate truth of the whole from individual examples. "I have always been in favor of examples," he said.

On the same day on which an intoxicated man from the Volkssturm accidentally fired a bazooka into the wall of Maria Szmaragovska's kitchen, the SS mined a nearby castle on a hill, and the wind that arose during the night tore up a window shutter tied with a mine and exploded the south front of the castle. A little while later the nearby farm building blew up and the three SS men involved lost their lives. Joseph stood at the edge of the road as they brought the bodies by.

An advance announcement read: "A column of Jews is passing by the farm building today." Many people gathered and waited. It was evening before the Jews came, walking along the edge of the road, tired and worn out. "They're blocking the street," said a guard. The woman innkeeper from the village wanted to give them bread to eat right beneath the window of the chairman and was prevented from doing so. Joseph stood by and experienced how the madness became reality. Alive, death passed on by him. Soon thereafter they died more innocently than had Allemann. Joseph knew one of the executioners.

90

The latter portion of the stanza carried the voices along with it. The end defined the battle between presence and disappearance. As if it had already been part of the beginning, it came with its sign and wrote them over the text that people had considered the truth. They did that because they had never learned to read. Now at the end when they maintained that they had not known anything about any of it, they joined in about having believed and not read, although there had only been one book for them. The power of the spoken word had grown out of the church and become the power of the public word. It clawed into the heart of the spirit and became its final manifestation. The spirit of the Movement captured the individuals, those who swarmed out enthusiastically to the freedom and bliss of their own possessions through the burst-open door, those dismayed by the fear and the rootlessness who let themselves be encircled and protected through the cast open door. In this artificial world they stood opposed to the collapsed world and believed they had found themselves again in the power and in the will that wanted to see the ruins and the movable stage props as the whole.

91

In the end no chaos arose. Only the existing world fell into confusion. Play stones were victorious, play stones fell over, but the games remained. Human beings love nothing more than the truth they have experienced once as truth. It never passes away and does not concern itself with the changing bodies. Truth is never over and does not allow itself to become undone and entwined in memory through guilt. The truth is the present, the hidden past is the rubble that covers the superiority of what is present. The power created history and the past for itself in order to hide itself behind the change.

In the final assembly of the Party functionaries, the headmaster is supposed to have proposed letting the outward appearances, uniforms, documents, and so forth continue to disappear, "for the essence remains."

Joseph saw the functionaries return to the people they formerly were. They descended from the stage and waited. The natives, who continued to play their game as before, who wanted to bring about by force what was impossible or actually believed that the deep wound was still capable of miraculous healing, were not able to take their leave from the stage of their meaning. They preferred to choose self-extinction in being nothing in death rather than being nothing in life.

The other was foreign to them or they were so seduced that the other did not even exist. "In the end psychology will prove itself correct," the grandfather said, when he died in fear a month before the end of the war and disappeared into the volcanic earth. "I have buried your ring," wrote Johann, "I don't want to see it again until peace returns."

The events blended into one another, became entwined, confusion of histories told the constantly similar history of destruction, of need, of hatred. In these moments every calling to a higher cause was a lie. Whatever loved itself tried to protect itself, and most people loved only themselves. Deserters hid in the woods and in attics, the law sought them. Returnees disappeared. The guilty crafted their innocence.

As if encased in amber, they waited out the end. The proximity of bloodletting banished the sadness of having belonged to the whole. Only the weather flag on the grandfather's glass hothouse turned. No jubilation arose for anything new. Happiness remained the hidden provision.

Establishing a hold, the denunciation, the hope of aligning oneself with the approaching enemy as well as with what they formerly were. The will to survive is the precondition for survival, for truth. The desire to undo what was done requires the plunge into secretive silence. The sudden rise of individual guilt is the ruse of truth. Nothing is more veiled than the truth.

92
His father moved the family to a safer place. There they achieved the end of the war, a few weeks later the father also joined them, and several months later for the first time they returned home together. There people had temporarily disappeared, then they were there again, and that everything was supposed to be new and different exceeded the ability to understand. What they "had" been, began immediately to ripen again as a lost ideal; the roots extended down into the counted recesses of the truth. The once fettered powers served the rebuilding. "For the most part nothing has happened," they said, "things will go better the second time."

During the first village festival at which those who had already returned home gathered together, the old familiar faces beamed beneath the glow of lanterns. "Grateful are we that we are still the old ones," one of them said. It is difficult to demand more of the dark, tenacious earth during the spring and of human beings on this earth than mere repetition of the same. Among the roast-chicken eaters and the roast-pork eaters, Joseph felt a hand on his shoulder. The nurse's friend was standing behind him and said with a grin, "Everyone eat what he can, get to it."

93
A few days before his departure for Abano, Joseph Algebrand walked along the linden path out to the fields. An early blast of cold air had set in on the leaves of the trees. The reddish brown confusion of color into which the broken

branches were hanging down, leafless and gray, made the end of the path seem brighter, as if emanating from a special source of light. To the left and right of the path stood brown corn stalks, ruffled by the harvest. The path, which stood out from among the fallen leaves, was overgrown with grass. It was hardly used any longer, as if it had already served its purpose as a path. The park behind it was overgrown, brush had filled the clearings, the ground had become swampy. In the crowns of the former favorite trees the sky hung lower; it was no longer the former sky that had been closer and more alive with signs.

When he left the tree-lined walk, Joseph stood in the fog, which the invisible sun made brighter and transparent. Here in the proximity to this place that had been a place of rest during his childhood, the cross had since disappeared, the lilac had grown wildly in all directions. Here during the second autumn after the war, also on All Saints' Day, he had again met Maria Szmaragovska. And he remembered having been shocked, as if she had betrayed the secret, her sudden disappearance.

"You have opened up the fir tree again," she said. "You should not blot out signs too early that reveal and conceal." She took him by the hand and led him across a long pumpkin field and pointed for a long time without saying a word at the yellow, rotting pumpkins which had been cut in two and were either lying there open or with their curves upward. Later, as they ran from furrow to furrow through the corn fields, threatened by the hardened leaves as if by scythes, she said, "This was the place of the skull, the heads are cut off, and nevertheless nothing has become any different; they stare at the truth, without eyes."

Now as before, most people were like the ghosts that they had been, thought Joseph Algebrand, and he heard Maria Szmaragovska's voice clearly; he saw the two of them going through the woods of alder, standing beneath the oaks. Pheasants ascended, chains of quail cooed across the meadows and disappeared again in the high grass. He heard Maria Szmaragovska's voice and language as untranslatable and his own language, which he had continued to speak, as a dead language he had had to learn as a language of inhumanity.

"I want to learn how to be silent," said Maria Szmaragovska, "too few people know what is hidden; they talk themselves into what is false, and then they gain control over it. They have turned what is evil into justice." "Do you want to avenge your suffering?" asked Joseph. "I lack the power to do it, I'm glad about that; this happiness is mine," answered Maria Szmaragovska, "here I will live my Poland."

Where the air-raid station formerly stood, Maria Szmaragovska and Joseph found a large hole filled with water; all around white turnips were growing, which were sprouting up poison-green leaves out of the loamy earth. "Like an empty grave," she said. "Where have the dead arisen? The resurrection is a curse." They continued across the fields, the soil stuck to their shoes, their steps became heavier.

Perhaps here the other path began for me, the wish for a world standing still, for a place without time. Joseph Algebrand and Maria Szmaragovska went crosswise into time, as in a story, in which everything has already begun, without anything new. The hare and the hedgehog were their companions. "May I seek syllables and talk into your truth?" he asked Maria Szmaragovska. "I've always wished that their truth would falter." She bent over and handed Joseph a piece of gravel. "Smash other stones with it."

If there has been progress, thought Joseph Algebrand, then it has been the fact that what is evil has become recognizable. In the country in which he had to live, what is evil had left its doors standing open, and what is evil came, cursed into an ideal, over the threshold. How often had he sat there ashamed, when he did not believe that what is evil was not of this world, that it could be excised. When he was sitting at the inn and followed the whirlwind of talk in which mostly the men unleashed their truths like dogs at a hunt, he felt the urge to shout along and beat on the table, "Man's nature is to be a fascist; in struggling against him, we learn freedom." But he preferred to listen to those who considered it possible to root out fascism, he feared that the terror had cast him too deeply into the dark and that the darkness was deceiving him. He saw nothing new, only the ghost of the opposing truth. But he was sure that no one had forgotten the past, rather that they had forgotten that they had forgotten how to be otherwise. They lived tenaciously, which kept them suspended in a present that spread into past and future. When he went with some of the students from the home to a Catholic home after the war, most remained what they were. Yes, it was almost worse, Allemann's wound festered beneath the scab of sin. The Movement regressed into a lurking calm. The headmaster gained in esteem, because he died in a prison camp; the director of the home was bored through by a pole which pierced his windshield during an excursion, as if an arrow had pierced him. Up until the end of school and his stay at the home, Joseph had always hoped he would get worms which he had had to combat because of Aunt Molly, who was betrayed out of her little hopes. But Aunt Molly remained close to him, up to her death, because she was the example of a victim. The rock to which she had clung was too hard. The script etched in her paled, and forgiveness opened up space in which he tried to protect those close to him, above all his parents, to whom he returned year after year at regular intervals, from the power of the transparent writing, above all when he caught himself letting the Movement enter beyond his borders and elevated it too much into the events that could dominate mankind. For a while longer he continued to walk across the fields, as if this walking was something worth preserving. It was perhaps the right that he took for himself, to set it down, to try it differently and to resist on this side of grace, coming to terms, judging, and understanding. The fields seemed neater now, their naturalness and unevenness had been smoothed over by machines. In spite of the monstrosity of the innovations, it remained the old land, the gray, uniform asbestos roofs that had replaced the tile roofs and the variations of their red color, made the houses blend in with the similarly colored earth. The roads were paved with asphalt, "We have the Führer's autobahn to thank for that," he had heard them say in the inn, as with everything else that had to do with the economy and progress. Thus in everything new the ashes were present.

Just as the fog broke up, Joseph Algebrand heard shots from the perimeter of the low alder forests, and out of the bushes and the corn fields hunters came. Since his father was still among them, Joseph Algebrand himself had disappeared among them. He turned around and went back to the path lined with the linden trees, then along it and around the park, as if he wanted to protect what was so close to him. He was afraid people might misinterpret his shyness. In his mother's presence so many things were alive there. How one was born became more vexing. Yet in a much different way, it was also present in Maria Szmaragovska, who was still alive and had not been shot because of Nietzsche's Zarathustra.

Joseph and Maria Szmaragovska continued on a bit farther. The stone in Joseph's hand became more familiar, and with this familiarity he walked next to her. "Once during the war you wanted to tell me the fairy tale about becoming human, about chaos and about cooking," Joseph said to Maria Szmaragovska. "We have time for that. As soon as you are done with school, you will eat at my place, and then we will have enough time to talk about what the hands of the cook betray about this game." "How did you survive the war?" asked Joseph. "Being unbound to the earth has rescued me, and when I am nearer to it, I will tell you about it. The time has not yet arrived for a person to move the cupboard from the wall which stands in front of that which does not show itself."

Joseph Algebrand now heard shots in front of him; there were hunts presently in progress everywhere. The shots seemed to move in a circle, and Joseph and Maria Szmaragovska also seemed to have gotten caught up in that circle. They crossed over a stream on whose banks ash and oak trees were standing; between them shiny red bushes were growing. A few hundred yards away they saw rows of people converging from the right and the left; on the one side hunters, on the other side the drivers, and behind them, half in the bushes, other hunters. Dogs barked, rabbits jumped up, pheasants flew up from the cover into the open. Rising steeply or surrounded by flying feathers, they fell to earth; the ones that got away seemed to leave the world. Joseph and Maria Szmaragovska remained standing. "Let's go on," Joseph urged. "We are going to stay where we are, at this point standing still is the right thing to do." The beaters and hunters gave signs. They were forced to move along. Then along the path they wanted to take, someone approached on an old woman's bike; hunched over, a man sat on it, with one hand he waved his hat and shouted with a laugh to the hunters: "I'm not going to turn around on your account." He rode up to the two of them, got off, and greeted Maria Szmaragovska, as if they had actually arranged to meet at this very spot. Joseph recognized the man; he had sold pelts before the war. Immediately after he had been drafted, he started acting in such a way that made people think he was crazy. It was a year after the war before he triumphed over the truth, was believed, and then released. "They don't even take me along as a beater," he said. "They despise me, but I wouldn't trade places with anyone."

Soon the rows closed in so much that the three of them had been encircled like the hunted game, only for them at this moment there was no escape.

Joseph Algebrand returned to his parents' house as it began to get dark. The house lay shrouded in fog that had settled in front of it on this day; the courage that was part of it to relinquish none of the suffering of the past marked a border that also passed through him and that he saw better in the dark than in the light. He thanked the steps which brought him safely to the door.

II

The memory of the funeral endured as pain. The massages altered nothing, the pain evoked no sorrow. The defining factor remained the crippling recognition of being among human beings who had been entwined around a wheel that was turning backwards; it pulled them back into what was lost in order to preserve it, or pulled them back in order to take righteous revenge for the horrors of what had happened. Both stood in the clutches of repetition. Death had lost its power, it plowed up nothing. The crippled present was victorious over the future.

Thick fog lay on the plain and blended with the contours of what was visible. Joseph proceeded on his way by car. He wanted to visit the grave of Eleonora Duse in Asolo. A guest had advised him to stop in San Vito on the way and to view the burial site of the Brioni family set up by Carlo Scarpa. He walked diagonally across the local cemetery. Through a low gate in the surrounding wall he entered the place that Scarpa had established. Green grass, little growth, and the concrete gray of the buildings formed from the white and the black of the concrete gathered together into an enclosed area. It was constructed like a conversation with death, without summoning any God. The paths, steps, flat areas, the area with water, the two sarcophagi facing each other, the plain chapel seemed to separate themselves from the symbolism, which the architect, who was buried under the side wall, hinted at, as if he were still prevented from creating the things independent of their interpretation and their meaning. They joined with one another in multiple ways in an emptiness, they drew the sky into it, the mountains in the north and the tree-lined walks beyond the walls. The birds flew back and forth during the intermezzo. The steps separating the buildings and their features, the most powerful sign of Scarpa's formalistic style, were steps toward death. In several moss had nestled in, here and there they were separated by cracks. They shunned any allusion to forgiveness, to the machinations of understanding. Life which had disappeared determined this style. At its border memory and future met, and time was the end of truth.

Afterword

Both within the confines of Austria and beyond, the name Alfred Kolleritsch is invariably associated with the eclectically progressive *Grazer Gruppe*, which emerged in the Styrian capital during the 1960s as a counterforce to those official literary and cultural forces emanating from Vienna, and as a counterpart to the more politically homogeneous *Gruppe 47* in the Federal Republic of Germany.[1] Born in Brunnsee in 1931, Kolleritsch studied history and German literature before completing a dissertation on Martin Heidegger and embarking on a teaching career in Graz. Simultaneously he became involved with the *Forum Stadtpark* and commenced his lengthy tenure as editor of its literary journal *manuskripte*. These defining activities have linked Kolleritsch closely with the continuing development of Austrian literature during his lifetime and remain his most recognized achievements.

Kolleritsch's initiatives in promoting contemporary authors through the *Forum Stadtpark* and his editorship of *manuskripte* are equaled by his own writing. As an author in his own right, Kolleritsch is best known for his poetry. The moderate tone and stylistic unobtrusiveness of his lyrical work, which has been described as "taciturn and tentative,"[2] often stand in sharp relief to the experimental nature and radical inclinations of modern, path-breaking authors with whom he has been associated, such as Oswald Wiener, Wolfgang Bauer, and Peter Handke. As a playwright, essayist, and novelist Kolleritsch is less well known, and perhaps less easily categorized. In English translation to date, only a small sampling of poems has appeared in several collections.[3]

Allemann is the third novel in Kolleritsch's extensive career. Published in 1989, the work—with its conventional narrative structure and ostensibly dated theme of life under National Socialism in Southern Austria—seems at first glance remarkably anachronistic. Yet the novel looms as prophetically timely when placed against the contemporary backdrop of the international attention surrounding Kurt Waldheim's wartime activities and the heated national debate over the radical Right's Jörg Haider and the FPÖ (*Freiheitliche Partei Österreichs*). This "seismographic" novel[4] casts a mindfully critical eye upon the present day as the author's semi-autobiographical account, narrated from the perspective of the protagonist Joseph Algebrand, correlates past historical events with the experiences of the present day in his homeland.

The opening passages of the novel provide a framework for the main body of the text, as a middle-aged Joseph attends a funeral that unleashes the flashback to his youth. The deceased, a prominent member of society, is intricately connected to Joseph's past: "Joseph visited him often because the man had the gift of making the past come alive in the present and of illustrating through his storytelling...that nothing from the past is truly past but rather that it just continues to repeat itself in one form or another"(5). Narrated in 1987 from Joseph's perspective forty-two years after the War, the account makes unequivocally clear that human nature and deep-rooted societal attitudes towards the events that shaped the course of Austrian and of world history have changed little over time. Like the periodic outbreak of evil in the nineteenth-century *Novelle* by the Swiss moralist and teacher Jeremias Gotthelf, *Die schwarze Spinne*, the festering of old wounds and the reemergence of latent predispositions in Kolleritsch's novel are grim reminders of the dualistic nature of human existence.

Contrapuntally to the now deceased businessman's "story-telling" and "version of history...that had remained unaltered by National Socialism"(5), Kolleritsch sketches his own personal account of history. It is implicitly transformed by those same events and expresses a broad range of reactions to the monolithic "storyteller" as well as to the hordes of official, semi-official, and civilian propagandizers, fabricators, and wittingly or unwittingly duped fellow-travelers of Nazi ideology who fill the pages of Joseph's life in the novel. The author's multifaceted approach can hardly be described as overtly aggressive or polemical in reopening the wounds from his nation's past. Far removed from the analytical, ideological eye of the historian, Kolleritsch's reflections rise to a realm of idealistic abstraction that supercedes the constraints of rational analysis. Like Maria Szmaragovska, the detained Polish cook who stirs her kettle of chaos-filled reality like a witch's brew, while calmly providing Joseph humanistic, philosophical insights into the truth, Kolleritsch gently blends fiction, reality, and autobiography in his artistic work.

Kolleritsch's resulting literary concoction remains complexly ambiguous and occasionally mildly sympathetic without being dismissive. The fact that the main character enjoys listening to the stories of the deceased, whom he otherwise despises, is but one indication of this viewpoint. Like Joseph, an idiosyncratic, Nietzschean-influenced seeker of truth and societal anomaly who seeks communion with the mysteries of nature, Kolleritsch, the sensitive artist, casts himself, for better or worse, into the cauldron that is his nation's past. The author's enduring idealism and humanism are tempered by the realities of a *condition humaine* that confronts stark historical fact. A letter Kolleritsch wrote to his newborn son around the same time in which he wrote this novel succinctly encapsulates a philosophy of life that ponders the idealism and uniqueness of human nature, but simultaneously acknowledges with calm acquiescence the limitations and shortcomings of that human condition: "We exist only in this one world, and the dividedness we experience is a part of this very world."[5]

The resulting proximity of good and evil, strength and weakness, courage and cowardice, is represented most strikingly in the irony surrounding Allemann. Amidst the novel's many examples of ambivalence, the title character himself is perhaps the primary one. Instructor Allemann shares Joseph's paradigmatic nonconformist, individualistic, and unconventional reading of history. Allemann, whose name connotes the "everyman" of the German "*jedermann*" as well as inclusive associations with "German" and "Germanness," himself becomes sacrificial victim of the stifling rigidity his Nazi affiliation demands of him. The hypothesized Aryan *Übermensch* erodes into the dreaded *Feindbild*, the contradicting image of whole classes of humanity (Jews, outsiders, the handicapped and mentally ill) that the Nazis sought to eliminate. Allemann's own idiosyncratic desire for genuine individual passion proved impossible within the rigid conformity and strict moral code the Nazis publicly promoted with popular organizations and widespread slogans. The unexpected inversions of power and passion are evident in so many ways within Kolleritsch's work. Ironically, Allemann's physical shortcomings (his club foot and poor eyesight) result from natural and hereditary causes, whereas the deformities of the other Nazis portrayed result from their military activities. With their missing limbs, eye patches, and prostheses, these officers hardly reflect the propaganda images of the virile Aryan. Ultimately they lack both the qualities of strength and joy that such organizations as *Kraft durch Freude* sought to idealize.[6]

Interestingly, Joseph's physical mark as outsider is neither hereditary nor war-related. Though his scar remains indelibly linked to far weightier realities, it resulted from a normal boyhood prank. When Joseph and his friend Johann happened upon an SS officer and his female companion in the woods of the Schlossberg, Joseph fell from the overhanging rock right in front of the naked, sexually aroused soldier. In the process Joseph gashed his thigh and received the scar that reminds Joseph later after the funeral years less of boyhood playfulness than of the historical events that shaped his life: "For the first time in quite a while he was aware of the long scar on his upper thigh, and the scar led him back to the wound, and it seemed to him as if there were nothing to remember but a present full of pieces torn off that spread out incessantly, and each one was simultaneously his past and his future"(12).

Hazy ambiguity remains a lifelong companion in Joseph's consciousness, as the scar on his thigh unequivocally reminds him in ensuing years. In developing the interrelationship between inbred attitudes and predispositions and the possibility and hope for change in the future, Kolleritsch proceeds on a poetic, suggestive, symbolic level. *Allemann* is neither a memoir of life at the front nor of inhumanity in the death camps. In fact, even though he references the horror and destruction of the War with a certain verisimilitude as it engulfed his own environment in its final years, Kolleritsch does not attempt to write history but, nevertheless, deals with its continuing impact on the life of his nation in his novel. Joseph's reflection at the beginning of the work manifests the author's standpoint of cautious wariness: "One does not illuminate what is vague and dark by explaining it"(6).

The novel is filled with obvious and obscure images and symbols. A central image is that of the youthful Joseph collecting the series of picture cards included in the cigarette packages of two contemporary manufacturers. One set comprises "pictures from the life of the Führer and the history of the Movement, the other the faces of German film stars"(29). As he eagerly collects the individual picture cards from his father, grandfather, and others, Joseph pastes them in an album with juvenile satisfaction. After considerable effort the boy eventually completes his collection, when a young, one-armed SS officer unexpectedly offers him the remaining missing picture that had long eluded him and his peers. Shortly thereafter, as the War itself extends to his Styrian homeland, the prized album is destroyed in a bombing raid along with the home where Joseph is a boarding student.

Joseph's persistent efforts to complete his collection are significant on several levels for the author's development of his character and plot. On the most general level, Joseph's efforts represent an impressionable young boy's natural inclination to participate in a youthful activity engaged in by his peers as well as his basic human need to feel part of a larger whole, both of the indigenous environment of the familiar surroundings of family and homeland and more ambivalently of the ever more pervasive grip of National Socialism. More specifically, Joseph's activity—one of many examples that could be selected from the novel—functions as a type of *leitmotiv* that ultimately allows the author to probe more deeply into the manifestations of National Socialism in everyday life and to illustrate his main character's passively firm aversion to and abhorrence of the phenomenon during and after the War.

Through his imagery—the ominous herons rising above a pond as symbols of the SS and Nazi presence, the green bars of RIP soap as reminders of the extermination of the Jews, and the fir tree with the open cavity at its base as Joseph's entrance into nature and higher realms of experience—Kolleritsch interweaves themes that bring personal experience to bear upon the ongoing process of encountering his nation's past. Within the context of Austrian literature, Austria's role in the events surrounding Hitler's rise to power and reign of terror remains an issue. The process of coming to terms with the past (*Vergangenheitsbewältigung*), which has had a comparatively longer history in Germany, has only of late seized hold fully in Austria. The emergence of Haider on the political scene and the worldwide impact of the Waldheim Affair may in many ways have proven to be catalysts for the deeper introspection Kolleritsch sought to elicit through his fiction among the population at large. Though other Austrian authors, such as the modern *Volksstück* dramatists and *Anti-Heimat* writers Mitterer, Turrini, Innerhofer, and Winkler, have long dealt in a radically polemical manner with the Austrian character, an atmosphere conducive to a broad-based public debate has not necessarily resulted. From this perspective Kolleritsch's semi-autobiographical novel can be viewed as a personal attempt to represent the phenomenon of National Socialism in his native land in a more specific way than do his earlier novels or his lyrical output.

The recent trend in historical research towards the

experience of the common man in everyday life (*Alltagsgeschichte*) and corresponding unearthing of the role that the so-called "average" German—or Austrian—played during the Nazi Era allows a reading of the novel against the silhouette of a number of recent historical publications, such as those by Saul Friedländer and Christopher Browning.[7] These historians offer complementary views on the degree of individual responsibility and culpability to be borne by the Germans and their Austrian counterparts, and through their nonideological, humane perspectives demonstrate that one does not have to subscribe to more radical theories concerning the "German" character or inherent ideologies of "eliminationist anti-Semitism"[8] to evaluate German and Austrian history from the focus of the common participant. At the same time, Friedländer and Browning, for example, clearly avoid the self-serving positions offered by modern-day right-radical groups such as Haider's and are united in their opposition to the blanket excuses of the "myth of the front soldier" and the image of the Germans/Austrians as "freedom fighters."[9] These open-minded historians continue to posit diverse, complex explanations for historical events.

The cast of characters in Kolleritsch's novel portrays all segments of society: Joseph's typical immediate and extended family, the local rural community, local governmental, political, and military authorities, and finally even the foreign prisoner-of-war soldiers and foreign workers, who were either forced laborers or recruits. The individuals within these groups display a wide range of attitudes, from staunch supporters to passive participants to unwilling participants and outright victims. Later during the funeral years, Joseph is shocked by the similarities that his contemporary society exhibits to this "historical" past. The manner in which this "outstanding" member of society is buried as a national hero with all the trappings of a National Socialist past on display, the native dress of the locals as indistinguishable from the uniforms of various military units, the deceased's widow reveling in the ceremony honoring her husband and standing at the head of a line of aging men displaying medals and distinctions from their tainted military past, and the words of the priest being overshadowed by the eulogies of the deceased's associates are all reminders of Austrian society's enduring contradictions and complexities.

Joseph's family itself is a microcosm of society. His father and mother initially support the Movement; his father participates by serving as an air-raid warden, although he is never fully committed to its most radical extremes and becomes increasingly disenchanted with its maniacally depraved uniformity. Joseph's mother represents the dutiful wife and loving mother who intuitively distances herself from the Movement, though not vocal in her opposition, as she follows her maternal instincts in protecting home and family. While little information can be gleaned about Joseph's two siblings, the figure of the maternal grandfather who lives with the family plays a central role. Though aging and increasingly feeble, the astute grandfather represents an enlightened view of the events transpiring. As a mentor who teaches his grandson through the voice of experience, the grandfather affects the latter's life in a positive way with the lessons he has gathered during his long life. The extended families of Joseph's two aunts and two uncles split into active supporters of the Movement and passive participants in the events erupting around them.

Through it all Joseph remains on the fringe of a family and a society he is intimately part of. The father-son relationship describes the give-and-take between opposing forces: "'Joseph, you're not going to have it easy,' said the father. 'You are being drawn away from the community. You are looking for the immutable, you only like something when it has a flaw, if others do not possess it in the same way. You are happy when a mushroom has a deformed double cap, when the trees are gnarled, when the fruit trees are covered with mistletoe and die off from it.... You were happy when you got a beating'"(26).

One of the main groups of positively drawn characters within the novel consists of the foreigners and prisoners of war living in Joseph's village. Maria Szmaragovska, the displaced Polish cook, is unexpectedly the most humane and humanistic of the individuals Joseph encounters. She reads Kant and Nietzsche in the small Reclam volumes Joseph brings her from his grandfather's library and hides the examples of rational philosophy and cultural critique beneath her skirts to avoid detection. She promises to tell Joseph the fairy tale of humanity when the war is over and a semblance of normalcy returns. Though caught by the authorities with Nietzsche's work, she is uncharged, apparently because the Nazis themselves appropriated the philosopher's ideas to their own misguided ideology. The revolutionary, vitalistic spark of genius, symbolized by the Polish cook's reading of the classics, for example of *Zarathustra*, is reflected in her name: Maria Szmaragovska is the emerald (*Smaragd*), the "gemstone" hidden amidst the unobtrusively ordinary. The piece of gravel she ceremoniously hands Joseph at the end of the novel with the words: "Smash other stones with it"(154) embodies her quiet, non-invasive activism.

The kettle Maria looks into as its contents boil and bubble reflects the chaos that Joseph and his world experience. Yet Maria is able to foresee calmly the "coming together" of the divergent ingredients and the eventual harmony that will result. It is Maria's promise to relate one day to Joseph the meaning of humanity in a fairy-tale that offers a glimmer of positive hope amidst the chaos, destruction, and death of the present day.

In contributing to the "new" [hi]story of Austria and National Socialism, Kolleritsch clearly portrays Austria as a pliable, if not willing accomplice, rather than as a victim of Nazi terror. Beyond the historical events of the 1930s and 1940s, Kolleritsch ties together the underlying mentality which not only paved the way for the spread of Nazi ideology in the first place, but which continued to fester in Austrian society in the late 1980s. The overall spectrum of societal rank and personal opinion that Kolleritsch portrays through the major and minor characters forms a composite of a whole, analogous to the album of individual picture cards that Joseph collects. The striking difference is that, while Joseph's collection of dubious images of idealized life under National Socialism is ironically totally destroyed in the bombing attack shortly after he completes it, the author's literarily-drawn composite picture of society endures.

---

[1] For background see *Die Geschichte der Literatur Österreichs.* Hrsg. Hilde Spiel. München: Kindler, 1976, 264-272.

[2] *Austrian Poetry Today / Österreichische Lyrik heute.* Ed. and trans. by Milne Holton and Herbert Kuhner. New York: Schocken, 211.

[3] See *Austrian Poetry Today* as well as *Contemporary Austrian Poetry.* Ed. and trans. by Beth Bjorklund. Rutherford: Fairleigh Dickinson University Press, 1986.

[4] Kolleritsch's first novel *Die Pfirsichtöter* (Salzburg, Wien: Residenz, 1972) bore the subtitle "Ein seismographischer Roman." The designation seems fitting for this novel as well.

[5] *Brief an Julian.* In *Prosa-Land Österreich.* Hrsg. Andreas P. Pittler. Klagenfurt-Salzburg: Wieser Verlag, 1992, 250. (My translation.)

[6] *Kraft durch Freude* was a primary Nazi social organization embodying the unity of the Movement. The organization's name became a popular slogan as well. See Joseph W. Bendersky, *A History of Nazi Germany.* Chicago: Nelson Hall, 1985, 166-167.

[7] Saul Friedländer. *Nazi Germany and the Jews.* New York: HarperCollins, 1997 and Christopher R. Browning *Ordinary Men.* New York: HarperCollins, 1992.

[8] Daniel J. Goldhagen's controversial *Hitler's Willing Executioners. Ordinary Germans and the Holocaust* (New York: Knopf, 1996) has promoted this viewpoint.

[9] For an analysis of Haider's position on these points, see Hans-Henning Scharach. *Haiders Kampf.* Wien: Orlac, 1992.

ARIADNE PRESS
Autobiography, Biography, Memoirs Series

Quietude and Quest
Protagonists and Antagonists in the Theater, on and off Stage
As Seen Through the Eyes of Leon Askin
By Leon Askin
and C. Melvin Davidson

On the Wrong Track
By
Milo Dor
Translation and Afterword
By Jerry Glenn

Unsentimental Journey
By Albert Drach
Translation by Harvey I. Dunkle
Afterword by Ernestine Schlant

Reunion in Vienna
By
Edith Foster
Afterword by
Heinrich von Weizsäcker

I Want to Speak
The Tragedy and Banality of Survival in Terezin and Auschwitz
By Margareta Glas-Larsson
Commented by Gerhard Botz
Translated by Lowell A. Bangerter

Choreography of the Heart
Stories about Love and Fulfillment
By Walter Sorell

Remembering Gardens
By Kurt Klinger
Translated by Harvey I Dunkle
Preface by Ernst Schönwiese
Afterword by Joseph P. Strelka

Night over Vienna
By
Lili Körber
Translation by Viktoria Hertling
and Kay M. Stone
Commentary by Viktoria Hertling

Thomas Bernhard and His Grandfather Johannes Freumbichler
"Our Grandfathers Are Our Teachers"
By Caroline Markolin
Translated by Petra Hartweg
Afterword by
Erich Wolfgang Skwara

When Allah Reigns Supreme
By Susi Schalit
Translation and Afterword
by Sabine D. Jordan

View from a Distance
By
Lore Lizbeth Waller

The Red Thread
By
Gitta Deutsch